The Caleb
Movement

Tamara C. Miller

To my big sis!!
 I love you so much! I appreciate
how you have been so supportive of
me. Thank you for being here and
know that I am always here for you

Love,
Jz

DEDICATION

Dedicated to all of those who, like me, were overlooked, considered "strange", "unusual", and "peculiar". God has need of every one of us...........

CONTENTS

Preface

Acknowledgments

PREFACE

Some have heard and discussed the story of Joshua in the Bible, concerning the Israelites and the "Promised Land". The Israelites had been slaves to the Egyptians for four hundred years. When the Israelites left Egypt under the leadership of Moses, God promised Moses that He was sending them to a land that was "flowing with milk and honey"; a land where they would prosper.

When Moses and the Israelites were close to the promise land, Moses sent representatives from each of the twelve tribes in which the Israelites were divided into, to go and scout out the land, assess the land, and bring back a report of their findings. Most of the men that were sent, came back with a negative report. While they saw that it was a prosperous land, they said that it was a place with powerful people; even stating that they had seen descendants of Anak there (Anakites were giants that were warlike people).

Out of the twelve men that Moses sent out, all but two, Joshua and Caleb believed that the Israelites would never be able to overtake the land. The other ten men sent were making statements such as "We seemed like grasshoppers in our own eyes, and we looked the same to them" (Numbers 13:33); the Israelites became afraid; that is until Caleb spoke. Caleb silenced the people by saying "we should go up and take possession of the land, for we are well able" (Num. 13:30).

Caleb was a man with a unique spirit that followed the Lord unconditionally. While the others were looking at their own strengths, abilities, and weaknesses, Caleb had faith in the God that he served, that with God all things were possible. He had no doubts that God was not only with them but would equip and empower them with whatever they needed to possess the land that God had promised them. Because of Caleb's unwavering faith and belief in the power of God, he could participate in taking possession of the promise land and receiving his inheritance.

In society, today, God is looking for individuals that are flawed and imperfect, but understand that where they are weak, He is strong, and who believe that all things are possible with Him. God is waiting for the people that are not afraid to go out and take possession of the land and declare to this nation and to this world that He is God, and that the saints are not afraid of the enemy. Though the enemy seems to be strong in number, God is mighty to save.

The Calebs of this generation may have suffered and had to overcome major issues, from depression, suicide, drug addiction, abuse (sexual, physical, mental, emotional, and verbal), body image and self-esteem issues; however, whatever issues they faced, they overcame them and are stronger for them. They are making a statement that no matter what battles they had to fight; they were the victors before their battles had even begun. The moment they turned their lives around, they started to thrive, and the more they share their testimonies with those who are dealing with the same issues, the freer they are, and the more they help others to be free; free from a life leading to misery, destruction, and possibly, ultimately death.

The Caleb Movement records the lives of individuals that have come from all walks of life but arrived at the same destination. It tells of how these individuals, though faced major challenges in life, believed that they were saved from their lives of destruction, to help others overcome their own battles. Maybe, just maybe, their stories can start a movement that will change a nation....

ACKNOWLEDGMENTS

I first want to give honor to my Lord and Savior, **Jesus Christ**, without which, I would not be here. Thank you, Lord, for giving me these books to write to bring deliverance and hope to a people that feel that there is no hope. I pray that every word that I have written will light the way that will lead someone to you. To my mother, **Brenda Watkins**, I would like to say thank you for always believing in me and never making me feel as though any dream that I had was too big or too great for me to accomplish. Thank you for always seeing what I couldn't see, until I was able to see it, too. To my sister, **LaTanya Cobb**, like my mother, you always pushed me to excel, always believed in me, and never let me give up. Thank you for being a nuisance. To my daddy, **Tyrone Watkins**, thank you for the discipline that you displayed every day, praying and studying your Bible. Thank you for instilling the word of God into me and giving me the foundation and the tools that I needed to succeed in this life. To my Brother, **Llonie Cobb**, thank you for challenging me to be better. Thank you for reading this chapter by chapter and giving me constructive criticism. I always want to make you proud. Thank you **Pastor Debrah Moyer** and **Prophet**

Justin Ruffin for speaking what God told you to speak, confirming these books and this movement. Last, but certainly not least, to my husband, my partner, my best friend, and my love, **Phil Miller**. Thank you for supporting me in everything that I set my mind to do. You have had to listen to every idea, every thought, every character, every story line, and you did so with such patience and grace. Thank you for being my rock. I love you with my life.

TAMARA C. MILLER

1 THE ROAD TO FREEDOM

Walking apprehensively towards one another, Princess and Bryce approached the dismal, dingy alley that wreaked of liquor and trash, at the same time. They felt strangely familiar with one another. Before they could properly address each other, several eerie looking shadows were casted upon the brick wall and they quickly realized that they were not alone. There were several others looking just as confused and bewildered as they were slowly, approaching them from behind. A couple of them, Princess could tell, came from wealth, by the shoes that they were wearing. One tried to dress in what some would consider "urban" attire, with a grey hoodie, jeans, and some boots, as to not bring attention to his financial status; however, Princess had seen enough guys with money come into the club where she worked, to know the difference. She loved labels. She knew about all the fashion designers, as she had always desired to become one herself, one day.

Bryce and Princess didn't know each other but they realized that they had seen one another from working on the same block. They were indirectly in the same line of work, so as they continued walking down that dark alley,

Princess felt a little more at ease as she trotted a couple of steps to get closer to him. At least he was familiar to her and amidst the rest of the individuals in that alley, she would rather stick with him, than to walk alone.

"Hey!" Princess said in a somewhat anxious tone. "Haven't I seen you around?" she asked.

Stunned and in disbelief that she would even recognize him, seeing as how he's been crushing on her since the moment he saw her "Y-Yeah. I'm Bryce and you're Princess, right?", knowing perfectly well who she was, but didn't want to appear too eager. "You work at the club, right?".

"Yeah, up on 23rd Ave. I knew I'd seen you before" she said. "How do you know my name" she asked curiously, looking up at him with a side-eye. Before he could answer, though, the others grew closer, so she abruptly changed the subject. "It looks like we're not the only ones heading in this direction. Do you have any clue what we're walking into?" Princess asked.

"I was just about to ask you that" Bryce responded. They were looking at all the others that seemed to be going to the same place; all walking very swiftly, as if they were trying to quickly get away from the others and looking over their shoulders. Some of them looked at Princess and Bryce with fear, as though they were going to rob them or something. Those looks weren't anything new; especially when it was clear that those same individuals had never been to this sketchy part of town before.

Walking a few paces behind Princess and Bryce, was Deni and Tony. It had been several weeks since they had seen each other at school and were surprised that they ended up there together. "OMG!!" Deni said in a hushed, but ecstatic voice. "What are you doing here, Tony? Did you get that crazy invitation, too?!' she asked.

"Yeah! Do you know what this is all about and why didn't you tell me you got one?" he asked.

"Why didn't you tell ME that YOU got one?" Deni shrieked. "We just haven't talked in a couple of weeks and it's been so much going on, that I haven't been able to tell anybody" she said. "I wasn't going to come because it just seems a little creepy" she looked around, grabbing Tony's arm as she heard more footsteps behind them. As she leaned in more, she whispered in his ear, "but it's exciting at the same time", she said with a little gleam in her eyes.

Deni liked this kind of thing. It reminded her of a scary movie. She turned around to see who was behind them and realized that there was a big scary looking, yet ruggedly handsome black man, tattoos covering both of his ridiculously muscular arms and a scar that ran across his cheek as if he had been slashed with a knife. He looked at Deni with a look of disgust; probably because she kept staring at him. A few steps ahead of him was a teenage girl, probably around eighteen or nineteen years old. *What is she doing down here by herself*, Deni thought to herself.

A few paces ahead of Tony and Deni was a white guy that looked to be in his early to mid-twenties. His jaw line was perfectly chiseled with a cleft in his chin, and his hair looked like it took him hours to perfect. He seemed as if he had a chip on his shoulder. There was also this beautiful Caribbean looking woman with bronze skin, long wavy dark brown hair, and cheekbones to die for. She seemed to have her own style, sporting a white t-shirt tied in a knot in the front, with colorful leggings and bright pink high tops. None of them seemed like they knew one another, but it seemed like they were all heading in the same direction….

2 THE STREET PHARMACIST

On the corner, in the heart of Strawberry Hill, in the city of Baltimore, stood Bryce Taylor; alone with nothing but his own thoughts to drown out the noise of the night. The sound of the roaring sirens, horns blaring obnoxiously, and the bass of the hip-hop music being blasted from cars that drove by in deafening volumes, had become the soundtrack of his nights; adding the fuel to his paranoia. Selling drugs, or being a "street pharmacist", as he liked to call it, was his business; his way of life and the only way that he could even imagine of getting his family out of the "hood". It wasn't always like this, though, he reminisced often, standing out there in the cold, staring off into the distance.

The memory of yelling and screaming from his parents, as he winced at the thought of the sound of the screen door as it was slamming shut, was the last memory he had of his father, John. Within a few hours, his, mother, Janice, had a phone call requesting that she come to the hospital. When she arrived at the hospital, she was informed that her husband had been tragically killed.

Apparently, a witness to the accident, spotted John speeding down the slippery, wet road from the torrential rain that was falling. Bryce knew that his father was speeding because he was angry about the argument that his parents had just had, because his dad never drove more than five miles over the speed limit; especially not in inclement weather. The witness stated that John hit a large puddle of water and his car hydroplaned before spinning out of control and down a ravine. It was the worst night of Bryce's life. His best friend, the one that understood him better than anyone, was gone; just like that. He never even got a chance to say goodbye.

Before the accident, John was Bryce's hero; taught him everything he knew. Bryce went everywhere with his father, did everything his father did, and wanted to be just like his father when he grew up; a man full of integrity, strength, and wisdom. To Bryce, John could do no wrong. John attended every baseball game he played, no matter how tired he was from working thirteen-hour shifts. He always made time for his son, but now, he was gone, and Bryce felt like he was left all alone.

Full of anger and grief, and not knowing how to cope, Bryce felt as though he was now left to pick up the pieces for everyone. He didn't even know how to deal with all his mixed emotions, himself; angry at God for taking away his father, and angry at his mom thinking that if she hadn't been arguing with him and ran him off, he would still be alive. At the age of sixteen, Bryce was left to be the man of the house, when he should have been still learning how to become a man. It was his responsibility now, to take care of his younger brother, sister, and their mother; at least that was the way he saw it.

After the death of Bryce's father, things became extremely different in their household. For months, Janice had found herself in a deep depression; barely making it out of her bed, unwashed with her unkempt hair that sat on her head, tangled, like a bird's nest. She never wanted to face anyone. Bryce's aunt, Jeanie, was the spokesperson for the family, handling the funeral arrangements, insurance policies, and bills for a while. She was John's eldest sister.

Janice had just become a recluse. She blamed herself for John's death. *If only I hadn't made him angry, maybe he wouldn't have left the way he did or at all,* she thought, often. Since Janice was unavailable to them, it was up to Bryce to make sure his siblings got to school every day. He also had to make sure his mother had food beside her bed, and someone to keep a watchful eye on her while he was at school, because he was afraid that she might try to harm herself while they were in school. Caring for his mother felt like a full-time job.

After about three and a half months Janice knew she needed help. Realizing she had to get out of bed and try to regain some sense of normalcy, for the sake of her children, Janice began to seek counseling which helped her to slowly return to her new reality. Bills were piling up, they needed food in the house, and she realized it was unfair to put all the pressure on her son, so she got two jobs; one as a waitress at night, and the other as an administrative assistant during the day.

Janice didn't have to work when John was alive. She stayed home and took care of the kids and the household. Unfortunately, the small amount of life insurance John had, and the money they had saved up, had quickly dissipated. Janice could no longer afford the mortgage by herself, so they had to move. All that she could afford was a two-bedroom apartment in what seemed, to her, to be an impoverished, seedy neighborhood. Although it was a rough neighborhood,

Janice found out shortly after moving there, that she would find the support and strength that she would need to go on, through other single mothers within the neighborhood.

The thought of getting his family out of Strawberry Hill overwhelmed Bryce's thoughts daily. He hated to see his mother coming home, taking off her shoes, and flopping down on the couch from pure exhaustion. Within minutes, a sound that would rival any bear, would come from her mouth; she'd be snoring, still in her work uniform. Bryce would just pick up her legs and stretch them out across the sofa and cover her with a blanket. That was their nightly routine.

With their mother working two jobs, and barely getting by, Bryce felt like it was his duty, as the man of the house, to make ends meet. Although his mom did everything she could to keep Bryce off the streets and keep him from living the lifestyle of those around him, she could tell that that lifestyle was starting to slowly draw her son away. She hated that John wasn't there anymore to give him that manly advice that he desperately needed. She did the best that she could, but she wasn't John. She didn't have the connection to him that his father had, and it was killing her.

When John was alive, he always kept Bryce on the straight and narrow. It was already hard enough growing up as a black man in this country. He didn't want Bryce feeding into the stereotypes that were already made against black teen boys. John knew the potential that his son had, and he did not want him to end up like he did; struggling for years before he started making enough to really have his family living comfortably. He wanted Bryce to get the education that he was not able to obtain, so that Bryce could get ahead sooner than he did. He wanted Bryce to follow his dreams and not just think big but aim high and achieve it; whatever his "it" was.

Two years had gone by, but John's words still resonated in Bryce's mind. Unfortunately, the more he got into the "game", the more those words started fading further and further into the backdrop of his mind, where he wanted them. *What good did all those words do me*, he would think. *As straight as my dad lived his life, and as hard as he worked, and as good of a man as he was, he still died too soon. All that hard work for what? Might as well take the easiest route.*

Bryce tried to get a job as a gas attendant at Royal Crowns, but he wasn't making nearly enough money to get them out of that neighborhood. He was still in high school and could only work a few hours after school. He thought often of just dropping out of school, but he couldn't let his mother or his father down by not graduating. That was the one thing he had always promised his father he would do, since neither of his parents graduated.

Bryce's mom, Janice, got pregnant when she was seventeen and John was eighteen. They were honor roll students, but just messed up by having unprotected sex one time, right before their senior year. Just one time was all it took for Janice to become pregnant. Janice's mother kicked her out and said she was a whore, that there was no way she was feeding another mouth, and that since she wanted to spread her legs open for John, John could take care of her. There was no way that John was going to allow her to be in the streets alone with his child, and his parents wouldn't allow them to stay there, unmarried, so John did the only thing he could do; get a job and rented a room for the two of them to stay in until they could get on their feet. John and Janice were on their own.

At first, they both worked at McDonald's. John at least wanted Janice to keep going to school and get her diploma, but once Janice started to get further along in her pregnancy, she started having problems and ended up being put on bed rest. She could no longer attend school or work. John had to work three jobs to support his family. After Bryce was born and Janice was physically capable, she found a neighbor to watch Bryce for a few dollars a week, while she worked a few hours to help take some of the pressure off John.

After several years working in construction, John finally became the foreman at his company and things became much easier for the family. The pay was good. That was when Janice could finally relax, stay home, and take care of their children. By then, Janice and John had given birth to two more children; Joseph and Bri.

Bryce remembered all the stories his dad had told him, as he was working underneath the car, or while they were fishing, about how he had to work his way up from the bottom because he had no high school diploma or degree and how difficult things were in the beginning for he and Bryce's mom. He wanted better for Bryce. It wasn't going to be much longer until Bryce graduated. He figured he would just keep selling until then, and then get a full-time job to help.

The money that he was getting was helping his mother. He couldn't wait until after graduation, so for now, this is what he felt like he had to do. In his mind, Bryce had no other options. He saw all the major dealers in the neighborhood in their expensive cars, expensive clothes, and living in their beautiful homes across town. That was the lifestyle he felt his family deserved to live.

Janice was afraid of the worse when Bryce started coming home with money, suddenly. He lied and told her he was doing odd jobs in the neighborhood and getting paid that way. She wanted to believe her son, but her mother's intuition was telling her something different and some of her friends in the neighborhood confirmed what was her worst fear.

Working so many hours, it was almost impossible for Janice to keep track of her son's whereabouts. All she could do was warn him every chance she got about how dangerous the streets were and how she wanted better for him and his siblings. She wanted them to graduate high school, go to college, and get great jobs; start their own businesses, even. She didn't want them struggling or depending on anyone and certainly didn't want them depending on the government like she had to.

Although his mother and father's words echoed in his mind every night he was on the corner, he couldn't let it stop him. He was on a mission. Determined to change his and the destiny of his younger siblings, he worked tirelessly but made sure he was home just before his mother got up to go to her second job at five o' clock in the morning. Although he was being rebellious for doing what he knew his mother didn't want him to do, he felt horrible lying to her. His mother and his siblings were all he had, and he would give up everything for them; even if it meant his freedom or his life. Little did he know, that was about to be put to the test.

One unforgettable, horrific night, Bryce was going through his usual conversation in his mind, rattled with guilt and torn between giving up this life and the money for the straight and narrow, when a black SUV, eerily crept by. The windows were like coal, the tint was so dark. It was impossible to see who was inside of it. Something just didn't feel right to Bryce, so in a panic, he started to turn to run, but before he could turn all the way around, he felt something stiff and cold digging in the back of his head. He knew it was a gun. He froze for a split second, and it felt like all the blood had just left his body. He heard a deep, husky voice utter the words "If you move, I will blow your head off".

Bryce didn't know what to do. He knew for sure that his life was about to end. He knew that if he tried to escape, he was dead. He tried to reason with the man. "Whatever you want, take it. Just please don't kill me", he pleaded. He felt a hand reach in his jacket pocket, taking his drugs and the money he had and then, suddenly, he felt an excruciating pain in the back of his head, and everything went black.

Waking up the next morning, his mother was standing over him with the most frightened look on her face. He was at home lying in his own bed. *How did I get home? Was that all just a bad dream; a nightmare to get me to stop doing what I was doing*, he thought to himself. The pain he felt in the back of his head when he tried to sit up, let him know that no, it wasn't a dream. It was, indeed, real.

Janice asked him how he was feeling and what happened to him. Afraid to tell her the truth, he lied and said that he was on his way home from doing some work and somebody pointed a gun to the back of his head and that's all he remembered. "Bryce Alexander Taylor, you tell me right now where you were, or the pain you feel won't just be in your head!" she bellowed.

Bryce knew that tone in his mother's voice. He knew that she wasn't lying, so he finally broke down and told her everything. Although he was afraid of what would happen next and if his mother would ever trust him again, it was a huge weight lifted off him to be able to tell her the truth.

"Bryce" she said in a mellow tone, "What did I tell you about those streets? I tell you all the time that the only way to get out of that lifestyle is in a jail cell or a coffin" she said, fighting back the urge to bawl and smack him in his head at the same time. "It was almost in a coffin, if that man hadn't found you and brought you home. I can't lose you, too, son". Finally breaking down, she sat down, put her head in her hands and managed to let out a weak "That would kill me, too".

Heartbroken by seeing his mother cry like that and knowing that he was the one that caused it, Bryce whispered in her ear as he kneeled down beside her, held her tight and said "Momma. I promise you, I will never scare you like that again." He didn't want his mother to be upset. That was the last thing he wanted to do.

After Bryce and Janice sat on the bed and he continued to hold her as she cried for several minutes, Bryce remembered something that she said when she was fussing at him. She said that a man brought him home. "Momma" he began to ask, "you said that a man brought me home?". With a confused look on his face, Bryce continued by asking "What man?"

"Some man said he found you lying in the street. He looked in your wallet and found your ID to get your address". Bryce faintly remembered being in a car and seeing the back of a man's head and seeing his eyes in the rearview mirror. It was something about his eyes that he remembered, that put him at ease, but that's all he could remember.

"Bryce, you are my first born. I want better for all my children. Why do you think I work as hard as I do? I want you to have the opportunity to get the education that you need so that you won't have to struggle like me" she reiterated. "I want you to be an example for your brother and sister." she said, gently placing her hand on his shoulder. "I know that we don't have much, but we're making it, son. The last thing I want you to do is die trying to take care of us". As Janice took Bryce's face in her hands and looked at him lovingly, she said "That is my responsibility, not yours. The only thing you need to do is to focus on graduating, going to college, and making a better life for yourself. Don't worry about us. We'll be fine."

Bryce took both of his mother's hands, placed them together, and gently kissed them. Although he heard those words, he thought to himself *you won't be fine. We're not fine, now.* He figured that this was just a minor setback; part of the game. He'd have to be more careful the next time. He wasn't convinced that they could make it without him doing what he was doing. It felt good not to have to worry about coming home and there being no lights, or food. It felt good to have a refrigerator full of food. It felt good to give his brother and sister money for things that they needed. How could he give that up? *I can't stop, now* he thought to himself.

Bryce pretty much slept that whole day and missed "working" that night. Unfortunately, he knew that whoever the guy was that knocked him out, stole all his money and his product. He was going to have to get that money back somehow, or things were going to get way worse for him and for his family.

As he was taking off his clothes, to take a shower, Bryce felt something in his pocket. At first, he got excited because it felt like money, but then he realized that it was some sort of black business card. The card only read: **101 Front St, NW, Baltimore, January 3, 2019 6:00 PM.** Completely baffled as he tried to remember where the card came from, he had a slight flashback of being in the back of the man's car that saved him. He never saw his face, never heard him speak, Bryce just knew he had this presence about him; not one to be fearful of, but one that gave him a peace he hadn't felt since his father was alive.

3 THE IMPERFECT PRINCESS

Unlike Bryce, Denise (AKA Deni) came from a very privileged lifestyle on the Eastern Shore of Maryland. She was a part of the Whitley Family; one of the most prominent families in the state of Maryland. Deni lived on a beautiful, plush estate with a sea of color flowing from the garden. There were horse stables with some of the most celestial horses anyone had ever seen, a beautiful lake that looked as though it were glass, an infinity pool overlooking the Chesapeake Bay, with a pool house/guest cottage, and a boat house. When driving through the colossal iron gates, it was like entering a fairytale.

Deni was stunning; the envy of all the girls in her school. Her long, luscious, raven colored hair swept down the middle of her back. Her skin was golden and had this radiant glow. She got her complexion and hair from her mother who was Greek. She was flawless. She had legs for days, and the best wardrobe that any teenage girl could ever want. Although Deni seemed to have everything, there was still a huge void in her life; she always felt alone.

Deni barely saw her parents. They were always working late hours, at the office, or out of town on these luxurious "business trips". Her parents, Jim and Clarrisa Whitley, owned one of the largest real estate development companies in the Delmarva region and had started to expand to the west coast. It was all about the money for them; being the best. Her parents were business partners, and even when they were home, they weren't present.

As an only child, growing up, Deni only had her nanny to ask questions about life. Her nanny, Lena, pretty much raised Deni. Although Lena was German and spoke broken English, somehow, she understood Deni perfectly; better than her own parents did; better than anyone. There were times when Deni would walk into a room without saying a word, and Lena knew exactly what was wrong with her just from her facial expressions. She considered Lena to be her best friend and even like a mother; the one she had always confided in, because she felt like neither her classmates or her mother could relate to her life.

Anytime Deni tried to talk about how lonely she was, her friends would say "What do *you* have to complain about? If we had *your* life, our lives would be set!" To Deni, however, her life was nowhere near what it seemed to be to others. She didn't know who her true friends were or who just wanted to be friends with her because of what they thought she had, making it very difficult for Deni to trust anyone besides Lena.

After Deni turned seventeen, her parents allowed her to stay home, often, by herself. She was a good student, very responsible and mature, and never gave them any trouble. They felt that there was no need to continue to pay a nanny anymore, since Deni was practically an adult and would soon be going off to college. Lena moved back to New York with her family, and there went Deni's only true confidant. Now, she would have no one to just be herself around.

Deni's parents were obsessed with appearances. Everything had to be perfect. They had to appear to be the perfect family; the perfect couple, the perfect parents, to the perfect child. Not only was Deni expected to be perfect, she was expected to look perfect, too.

Her parents worked out every day; Jim running at least three miles a day, and Clarissa playing tennis with her friends on their indoor tennis court. They made sure they kept in shape and they wanted to make sure Deni stayed in shape, too; especially Clarissa. Deni could always hear the shrieking sound of her mother's voice, like nails scratching a chalkboard, every time she ate, saying "A moment on the lips, forever on the hips".

As a child, Deni was a little on the chunky side, which was an embarrassment to her mother. She didn't want people thinking that they were the kind of parents that had a lazy child that sat around eating potato chips and fast food all day. Clarissa was so embarrassed by the few pounds of baby fat that Deni had put on when she hit puberty, that she forbade anything of pleasure, food wise, from entering the house. Deni never got to enjoy birthday cake, ice cream, fast food, or anything that normal kids enjoyed, that is, until they started leaving her home alone.

With no one monitoring her eating, Deni would sneak food into the house and binge eat, devouring all the food that she wasn't allowed to have; cookies, pizza, chips, whatever she could get her hands on. She was like a caged animal that had been starved for weeks and had finally been released. After scarfing down all the food, she would lean over the toilet, stick her finger down her throat, and rid her body of the calories that she figured she'd gained by eating it. Overcome with so much guilt, shame, and anger afterwards, she would just lie in her room and cry. She felt as though no one would understand what she had to go through.

She felt so out of control. Her parents could never know the secret that she was hiding. She couldn't let them know that their perfect daughter was so imperfect. *They wouldn't care anyway* she thought to herself. *All they cared about was keeping up appearances for the sake of their business associates and "so called" friends* she thought.

During Deni's first year at college in Miami, she thought that she would no longer have to binge eat. She would have the freedom to eat what she wanted, when she wanted, and that's exactly what she did. All the junk food was so easily accessible to her. She realized in college, that most of the students had a crappy diet. *Finally,* she thought to herself with a blissful smile on her face, *I'm free.*

Although, at first, it was difficult for Deni to meet new people, she decided that she was going to join the dance team, which opened opportunities for her to meet her new best friends; Daisy, Kara, and Tony. She was at one of the most prestigious universities and most of the students came from well-to-do families, so they could easily identify with her. They had the same or very similar stories about their parents; barely home, keeping up appearances, they could even identify with determining who wanted to be their friends for them, or for what they had. She finally felt understood.

Things were going well for Deni at college. She did, however, start noticing a slight weight gain. It was only a few pounds, and yeah, her clothes were a little snug, but she could still fit into them, so she didn't think anything of it. She just thought she'd workout a little; no big deal. She was happy, and Daisy and Tony always complimented her on her figure and how great it was. They had even made statements that they would kill to have a body like hers. She was starting to have curves in all the right places and the guys seemed to really take notice of and appreciate them. For the first time, Deni felt good about herself, but all of that was about to change.

It was time for the Christmas break. As soon as Deni's driver's car hit the Chesapeake Bay Bridge (her parents were too busy to pick her up), she started to feel a panic overtake her; a very familiar feeling. Her hands started to shake, she started sweating, and she felt as though she couldn't breathe. She felt like every mile she got closer to home, the more she felt her freedom leaving her and the more stifled she had started to become. It was as if she was a little child again. Suddenly, those few extra pounds she had put on that she didn't worry about at school, started feeling like one hundred pounds. She knew her mother and dreaded seeing her.

The moment that Deni walked through the door at her house, she saw her mother walk around the corner with a long charcoal gray cardigan, a navy and white striped t-shirt, some dark denim jeans, and charcoal gray booties. Deni couldn't believe how radiant her mother looked at the age of fifty-four. She looked better than ever. *How is that even possible,* Deni thought. Clarissa's dark wavy hair, which had one perfect sliver of silver placed perfectly in the middle, never seem to be unkempt or ever out of place.

The look on her mother's face turned from excitement in seeing Deni, to disgust from looking at her. "Deni, what have you done to yourself" Clarissa gasped in disbelief, placing her hands over her mouth. "You've gained so much weight", and just that quickly, there it was. Deni felt that old familiar feeling of "not good enough" sink in.

Deni had always felt like she let her mother down, when it came to her looks. Clarissa always had something negative to say; especially when it came to her weight and her body. She always bragged about how she's stayed the same size she was since she was in high school, because she took such great care of herself, and worked out every day, as if Deni was such a lazy slouch. Clarissa often criticized Deni for not working out with her. The truth is, she didn't mind working out; it was the working out with her mother that she wanted to avoid.

Christmas dinner was the worst. All the family came over, and they all talked about how much weight Deni had gained. Having her grandmother there was like having Clarissa in surround sounds. The two of them criticized everything she ate. Her grandfather, George, could tell that she was uncomfortable. "Ease up on the girl! Good grief! You two act as if she's five hundred pounds or something!" Deni could always count on Grandpa George to help her out. He was the only one that seemed to care about her. She wished he lived closer, so she could spend more time with him, but Connecticut was too far away. Besides, she couldn't see him without seeing her grandmother.

Counting down to the days that she could go back to school, Deni tried to avoid dealing with her mother as much as possible. Jim wasn't as bad as her mother, but she didn't have much of a relationship with him, either. Even when he was home, he was on his phone, on his computer, doing paperwork; always locked away in his office doing something for the business. They never did anything as a family, unless it was to put up appearances at some dinner party for her parents' associates.

She hated being home, again. At school, she was so happy. Now, it was just like being back in prison where the warden controlled everything. The desire to binge eat came back, again. This time it was worse than before. When she got back to school, she continued to purge after eating, for fear that she would gain weight again.

After a month of being back at school, her friend Daisy, started to notice that every time Deni ate, she immediately went to the bathroom. One day, Daisy decided to follow her to see what was going on. Deni didn't know that she was being followed until she heard Daisy's voice.

"Deni are you ok?" she asked.

"I'm fine" Deni replied. "I think the food just made me a little sick. That's all". Her next question was a little more personal.

"Deni are you pregnant?" Daisy asked with a concerned tone in her voice.

Taken back by her question, Deni yelled at her "No! I'm not pregnant! Now leave me alone!".

Realizing that she had pushed the wrong button, Daisy reassured her that if something was going on, she could talk to her about it. Deni further insisted that she was fine, so Daisy left. It never left her mind though, and now Deni felt even more ashamed that she had been caught, and that she lied to her best friend.

As the days went by, Daisy kept a watchful eye on Deni, but Deni knew she had to be more careful in hiding what she was doing. The effects of all the purging and excessive working out, was starting to take a toll on her, though. She started to get too thin and too pale.

When her friends asked her if she was on a crash diet or if she was feeling well, she would just joke and tell them that maybe she had been hitting the gym a little too hard and maybe she needed to chill out, a little. She told them that she was using the gym to work out some frustrations she had been having.

Daisy grew more and more concerned and finally made the decision to confront her again. This time, she wasn't going to let her get off the hook so easily. She was prepared for any backlash that Brandi would have given her. Daisy wasn't about to back down this time.

"Deni, I think I know what's going on with you and I want you to know that I don't judge you" she said as she placed her hand gently on her shoulder, looking directly into her eyes. She wanted Deni to see that she meant every word of what she was saying. "I love you, and you don't have to go through this alone" Daisy pleaded, "just please let me help you".

"You don't know anything about me" Deni bellowed, as she snatched her shoulder away. "There is nothing wrong with me. I told you I was fine! If I wasn't, I would've told you, now leave me ALONE!!" She stomped off with her arms folded. Daisy knew for sure that something was terribly wrong with her friend and had no clue how to help her. It was killing her to watch her friend change so drastically, and so quickly. It scared her.

After that incident, Deni started to withdraw from her friends. She no longer smiled, and her grades were starting to plummet because she didn't even want to come out of her room and be seen. She was so ashamed of herself for allowing herself to succumb to the pressures of her mother, again. She felt like she was at the lowest point in her life. She thought about the summer break that was coming soon, and the thought of going back home again was more than she could handle. As she was sitting on the floor in her room, with a blade to her wrists and as she started to dig the knife in, there was a knock on the door.

Suddenly, a card slid under the door. She quickly jumped up, ran to the door, and swung the door open, but there was no one in sight. Confused and baffled at how they disappeared so quickly (there was only one way in and one way out at the end of a long hallway), she reached down and picked up the card that was left at her door.

Deni couldn't explain it, but at that moment, she felt such a peace, unlike anything she had ever experienced before. She immediately threw the knife down and began to weep, but not tears of pain or depression, such as what she had been crying before. This time, Deni's tears were tears of gratitude and gratefulness. It was at that moment that she realized that she had so much to live for. *Who left that card,* she wondered?

4 THE SEDUCTIVE STRIPPER

From the outside, Princess was unlike any other stripper or exotic dancer. At the age of twenty, she had all the right curves, the sex appeal, and eyes like pools of caramel that men just got lost in. There was something about those eyes and those pouty lips that brought men to their knees at her command. She knew exactly how to work them. She knew how to get exactly what she wanted from them, and what she wanted, all she wanted was their money. Somehow, Princess made every man in the club feel as though she was putting on a performance for one; like no one else was in the room.

Although most of the exotic dancers at the club wanted to be like Princess, they secretly hated her. The nights she danced, were always the busiest nights because the men, and a few women, all wanted to see her. She always had the most private dances (which was where the real money was); she was always asked to be in the VIP section when entertainers or celebrities came into town and visited the club. She was everyone's favorite at the club, and the owner, Rick, especially loved her because the more attention she got and the more guys she brought in, the more money he made.

Rick always gave Princess special attention, which caused the other girls to be even more jealous of her. Rick was an ex-pro football player, and owner of the club. Rick looked like a football player, too. He had bulging muscles, a broad back, and thighs that looked like they could crush cement blocks between them. He was tall, dark, and extremely handsome. Every girl at the club wanted Rick, but he only seemed to have eyes for Princess.

Rick was the kind of man that people did not say "no" to, but Princess did, repeatedly. She wasn't interested in guys like Rick. Besides, he was her boss. Princess had a no fraternization rule. She did not believe in getting into relationships of any kind with those with whom she worked with or for. She wasn't impressed with his money or his looks. He was arrogant, a chauvinist, and thought he was every woman's dream; however, Princess needed the money that she was making, so she had to "play nice" with Rick. She was afraid of him, and she needed the job to take care of her daughter that no one at the club even knew she had.

Princess was a very private person. No one knew that the person that they saw on stage every night was a totally different person when she got off the stage and walked out that back door. No one at the club knew much about her; where she lived, where she was from, or anything personal. She liked it that way. She was very protective of her daughter, Nylah, and wanted to shield her from that lifestyle as much as possible. She didn't want Nylah to go through what she had gone through, as a teenager. Princess would do whatever was necessary to make sure the same thing that happened to her, wouldn't happen to Nylah.

When Princess (AKA Kimberly) was sixteen years old, her life seemed to be going along just fine. She was raised in a good Christian home with both of her parents; she was an honor roll student, and one of the captains on the cheerleading squad. She had a great relationship with her parents; especially her father, Jesse. She was a daddy's girl; the apple of his eye.

Kimberly was a virgin; a sweetheart, and the desire of most of the boys in her high school. Her new boyfriend, Matt (a senior), the captain of the football team, made her the envy of every girl in school. He had rippling muscles, the prettiest hazel eyes, and dirty blonde, curly hair. Matt was beautiful and was a perfect gentleman to Kimberly; at least he played the part well. He always made sure to be respectful to her parents, opened the door for her, pulled out her chair, and anything else that a true "gentleman" would do. It was one weekend that changed the whole protectory of Kimberly's life.

The school's football team, the Mavericks, had a big game coming up, and everybody was excited. It was the biggest game of the year; state championships. There was talk about a huge party after the game at one of Matt's teammate's, house. Normally, Kimberly wasn't allowed to go to those parties because there had been rumors of underage drinking and illegal substances distribution going on; however, this time, because Kimberly's parents knew

Matt's friend's parents through church, they decided that it was okay for her to go.

The excitement from the game spilled over to the party. The team won the state championship. It was the first time in almost fifteen years. Matt wanted to celebrate, and in more ways than just being at the party.

Matt took Kimberly to the pier by her house. He said he just wanted to be alone with her and that it was too crowded at the party. After he parked his red mustang convertible, he told her how much he loved her, how special she was to him, and how he wanted to show her just how special she was. He pulled out a small black box. Inside the box was a beautiful gold necklace, with Matt's class ring on it. She turned around and pulled up her thick tresses so that Matt could put the necklace around her neck. After that, they started kissing.

Matt's kisses were always sweet and soft, and sent a warm tingling feeling down her spine. Normally, she loved his kisses, but on this night, something was different. He started to kiss her harder and became more aggressive. He had been amped up since the game and she didn't like the way he was behaving, so she yelled at him. "Stop!" as she snatched her skirt back in place and pulled her top back down.

"You know you want this" he said, as his hand started heading towards the inside of her thighs, again. "You've been stringing me along for months, now. You had to know it was going to come to this. Don't be a tease!" he shouted, all the way on top of her at this point.

Matt was too strong for Kimberly to fight off. He forced himself into her, pounding on her until he finished. Afterwards, while he fastened his clothes, Kimberly opened the door of the car and ran. She never wanted to see his face again. When she got home, her parents were asleep in the living room on the couch.

Kimberly ran straight to her bathroom, took a shower, and never told anyone what happened. She felt dirty and ashamed. She tried to think of what she had done to deserve that. *Did I lead him on? Was I a tease*, she thought to herself? Trying to put it out of her mind, she just pretended that it never even happened.

A couple of months had gone by and she hadn't talked to or even looked at Matt. When she saw him coming down the hall at school, she would turn the other way and go in the opposite direction. He acted like nothing happened, of course. That night he left her a threatening message warning her not to say anything; telling her that if she told anyone, no one would believe her. Matt was the town hero; the boy next door. She was nobody until she started dating him; at least that's what he made her think.

After about a week, Matt had moved on to another girl, which Kimberly was happy about, however, she was somewhat afraid for the girl. *What if he does the same thing to that girl as he had done to her, she asked herself.* Kimberly had more to worry about than that, at this point. She had tried to move on, but something was different about her; she could feel it. The more she tried to pretend that nothing was wrong, the more that she knew something wasn't right.

After several weeks of vomiting and feeling nauseous every morning, the slight cramping in her stomach, and the extreme fatigue she felt, Kimberly was horrified to think that her worst nightmare had come true.

After missing her period that month, Kimberly was deathly afraid of what her body was trying to tell her. She didn't want to get a pregnancy test, but had to break down and get one, just to be sure. Too many girls in her school were pregnant and she knew what that was like for them. Anxiously sitting in the school bathroom (she couldn't risk taking it at home) on the toilet, she was praying hard that the test would be negative, although she knew in the back of her mind, it wouldn't be.

Positive; the results she was dreading seeing. *What am I going to do, now? How am I going to tell my parents?* were the thoughts that plagued her mind for weeks. Luckily, she wasn't showing for a while, so no one could tell she was pregnant for the first six months.

During the seventh month, however, she started showing. Everybody at school started to wonder why Kimberly started wearing big sweatshirts, t-shirts, and baggy pants. That was never how she used to dress. Before, Kimberly wore clothes that would put her hour glass figure on display. That was what made the boys go crazy for her. She had become withdrawn, distant, and for the most part, a recluse. She didn't know who she could trust or what people would think of her when they find out that she was pregnant. She started to become severely depressed.

Kimberly's friends started noticing the drastic changes in her. Her parents started noticing, as well. It was inevitable. *Someone was going to start asking questions* she thought to herself, and that's exactly what happened. Her parents sat her down at the dining room table, and said, "Kimberly, we're very concerned about your behavior lately. You just haven't been yourself". As her mother, Dawn, placed her hand lovingly on top of Kimberly's tightly clenched hands, she continued "You don't want to be with your friends anymore; you stay locked away in your room" Dawn questioned, with a concerned look on her face. "What is going on?"

Kimberly just started to cry. She couldn't hold it in anymore. She knew that the one person that knew her better than anyone would be her mother and she could never lie to her mother. Anytime she tried to, her mother would know it, so she just told her "I'm pregnant" and just froze. She couldn't believe that she let those words come out of her mouth or that they were even true. She was terrified about what was about to happen next.

Jesse overheard her mother Dawn repeat that Kimberly was pregnant and he quickly became enraged! He jumped up out of his seat, pounded his fist on the table, and started yelling and screaming, asking her how she could do something like that. "How could you be out here behaving so loosely and frivolously" he shouted as he raised his hand to slap her, but quickly withdrew his hand. Jesse brought the volume of his voice down, as he took a deep breath.

With tears in his eyes, almost whispering, he let out "No daughter of mine would go out and get herself pregnant. Do you even know who the father is?" he asked as he looked at her in pure repulsion.

In disbelief, Kimberly clutched the collar of her shirt with a look of bewilderment on her face. She couldn't even believe her father would ask her something like that or that he was talking to her like that. She didn't know who that person was because to her father, she could do no wrong. It crushed her that she broke her father's heart, but what hurt her even more is that he thought she was just some promiscuous little slut, sleeping with the entire neighborhood. "Kimberly, I am so disappointed in you. I can't even look at you. I don't even know who you are" he sobbed as he walked out of the room into the hallway, leaning up against the wall.

Jesse couldn't bring himself to admit the real problem. It was the fact that this was his baby girl; his perfect princess, had "been with" a boy. The thought of some boy having sex with his daughter and getting her pregnant was more than he could handle. He felt like it was his fault; that he somehow failed her as a father, but he could never admit that. His pride wouldn't let him.

Kimberly didn't want to be in that house anymore. She didn't know what she was going to do, but she knew she couldn't look at her father anymore. It killed her that she disappointed him like that.

Kimberly packed a bag, left and never looked back. She wandered around from town to town for the first month, sleeping in shelters and getting food from the different soup kitchens at local churches. The next month, Kimberly had Nylah, and she was all alone. She found a program that helped find shelter and resources for new, homeless mothers, to help them become self- sufficient.

The program, The Dinah House, was a lifesaver. For the first couple of months, Kimberly and Nylah were doing well. Kimberly had to quit school because she had nowhere to live, for a while. The program was helping her take classes at night to try to get her high school diploma, but when Nylah was about a year old, The Dinah House had to close because they no longer had the funding to keep the program going. Kimberly was going to be homeless, again….

Unfortunately, Matt wasn't the last man to rape or sexually assault her. Living from shelter to shelter and literally on the streets, before Nylah was born, was dangerous. Sometimes she would sleep with men to get some money to try to feed her and her daughter, but she hated doing that, with a passion. Many times, Nylah was in the same room while Kimberly was servicing a man. She knew she had to find a way out of that, quickly. Nylah was growing older and that was something she could not live with, but Kimberly refused to go back to her parents' house.

Not looking where she was going, Kimberly ran into this lady in the mini market, just around the corner from one of the shelters that she frequented. "Hey! Watch where you're going!" shouted the lady. Kimberly looked up and there stood this tall statuesque beauty. She had long, red, wavy hair, and her makeup and skin were flawless, with her bombshell red lipstick completing her sultry look. She had on a mixed brown and black quarter length fur jacket with a slinky black dress, black fishnets, and black stiletto heels.

The lady looked down at Nylah and said "Aren't you a cutie" as she patted Nylah's big sandy brown curls. Kimberly pulled Nylah close to her and apologized to the lady for bumping into her. "Hey" the lady yelled, as Kimberly hurriedly started walking towards the door. Kimberly turned around, and the lady asked where she was headed and if she needed a ride? "It's too cold outside for you to be walking around with this baby".

Beyond the lady's outward appearance, there was something about her that just seemed to make Kimberly feel as though it would be safe to go with her. She had a warmness in her eyes that Kimberly hadn't seen in anyone's that she'd encountered, lately. Besides, she couldn't be any worse than any of the men that she had already encountered, who called themselves helping her. Kimberly knew what kind of help they were trying to offer her and the price she would have to pay to get it. "Yes ma'am" Kimberly responded to the lady, she and Nylah moving closer to her car, "We could use a ride".

Kimberly and Nylah climbed in the lady's red convertible Mercedes Benz. The beige leather seats were plush, and they were heated, too. "They call me Ginger" the lady finally introducing herself and asking, "What's your name, Princess?"

"My name is Kimberly, and my daughter's name is Nylah".

"Funny, you don't look like a Kimberly. Where do you live?" Ginger asked, as she looked back and forth between Kimberly and the road.

As Kimberly put her head down, in shame, she lowered her voice and said "We live in a shelter, right now; only until I can get on my feet. I'm looking for a job, but it's hard out here without an address or a high school diploma, you know?".

Kimberly had always felt like she was disappointing Nylah, because Nylah had never known stability or having her own place to live. Ever since Nylah was born, Kimberly had her moving from place to place, never knowing how long she would be there. It broke Kimberly's heart that this is the kind of life her daughter had grown accustomed to.

"I may have something that may be perfect for you. With a little tweaking, you could pull it off. You have the goods. The pay is good. If you're good at it, which with my help you'll be unbelievable, you can walk away every night with at least $1000-$2000".

"$1000-$2000 a night" her high-pitched voice screeched out loud, eyes were as big as saucers. "I'll do it, whatever it is; anything to get me and my daughter out of this situation". Little did she know what she had signed up for.

That night, Ginger decided that she didn't want to see Kimberly and Nylah in another shelter. Ginger said that Kimberly reminded her of herself when she was her age and understood what it was like to be on the streets with a child and nowhere to go, so she let the two of them stay with her for a little while; until she could get on her feet and find her own place. Ginger did not want another girl to be living the way that she used to have to live; especially not a girl like Kimberly. Life on the streets was dangerous; especially for a young girl like her that seemed like she had no street smarts and didn't come from that kind of life.

The next morning, Ginger and Kimberly took Nylah to the drop-off daycare center that Ginger was an owner of, and she took Kimberly to see her business partner, Rick. When they pulled up to the parking lot, Kimberly was somewhat shocked to see where they were, but now it made sense why Ginger was dressed the way she was dressed when she first met her.

When they walked in the door, all Kimberly saw was half-naked women, gyrating on the stage, and men as well as a few women, getting lap dances. She wasn't sure this was what she wanted to do, but what was the alternative? At least as a dancer, she didn't have to have sex with the men; all she had to do was dance, right? At least that is what she told herself.

Walking up to this huge body builder type man, with his shirt opened and his pecs showing, Ginger kissed him on the cheek and said "Rick, this is Princess" as she motioned for Kimberly to come closer. "She's interested in a position here. I told her that I would introduce the two of you and see if you thought she was a good fit for the team".

"Well, well, well" Rick responded, rubbing his hands together, looking her up and down with that sly as a fox grin on his face; like she was a 4-course meal. "Look what we have here. You are perfect for our team. I see a diamond in the rough", taking his index finger and outlining her face (which was making Kimberly's skin crawl).

"With a little help from my partner, Ginger, you could be one of the best dancers this club has ever seen". Rick slowly turned her around as if she was a rotisserie chicken on a spit rod. "You're hungry. I can see it in your eyes. I need someone with your potential on my team". He looked at Ginger, grinning from ear-to-ear, and said "I see why you brought her here. That's why we're business partners. You bring me the girls, and I make the magic happen". He put his arm around Ginger's waist and kissed her on the forehead, never taking his eyes off Kimberly.

Ginger smiled at Kimberly, now giving Kimberly her new name, Princess, and said, "I knew you would shine" and winked at her. That reassurance from a woman, that seemed to be living the life, was all she needed. She would do anything for her child and she felt like Ginger would be able to show her the ropes and protect her at the same time; and Ginger did.

Ginger became Princess's Fairy Godmother; at least that's how Princess saw her. It was Ginger's idea for Princess to keep her private life separate. No one knew about Ginger's daughter, either. She shielded her daughter from that lifestyle, as well. Besides, she thought that Princess would be less desirable to men, if they knew she was a mother. The men that came in their club looked at these girls as their fantasy; mothers were not a part of that fantasy.

Ginger paid for Kimberly to take dance classes and advised and prepared her for what she was about to embark upon. Ginger told Princess to never allow any of the men to get too close to her. She encouraged her to talk to them and make them feel comfortable with her, when giving lap dances, but at no time was she to tell them anything personal about her; not even her real name.

Ginger taught Kimberly how to save and invest her money, as well, knowing that this was something that she did not want to be doing and couldn't successfully do for the rest of her life. There was a good five-year window for dancers. After that, there needed to be something else to move on to.

The first night that Princess had to dance, she felt like she was going to lose it. She was nauseous, sweating profusely, and shaking uncontrollably. Ginger gave her a shot of Hennessy, which Princess quickly swallowed, although she never had any alcohol before, to settle her nerves and take the edge off. She also gave her a few puffs of weed.

"It's ok, Princess. Everyone feels like this on their first day". As Ginger rubbed her back soothing her, and as the Hennessy and weed started to slowly provide a warm sensation through Princess's body, relaxing her, she reminded Princess, "these men are here to see you. You want them to go home dreaming about you every time they see you on that stage".

As Princess heard herself being called to the stage, she looked at Ginger that took her, dressed in nothing but a G-string and a beaded bra and stilettos, by the hand and walked her out. She whispered in her ear "You're going to be just fine. Just relax and give them a show that they'll never forget"; and that is exactly what she did.

It was as if Princess was another person. That was the moment that Princess really became a woman. She felt like for the first time, she was in control of her sexuality, her body, and her life. *This time*, she thought to herself, *I am going to control these men, instead of them controlling me.*

Once she realized that the more she became their fantasy, the more money she made, she was all in. She became a pro at knowing which men she could get the most money out of; the ones that looked like they could never get a woman any other way. She became exactly what they wanted; stripper royalty. She lived up to her name. Unfortunately, that expertise got her the attention from a lot of the wrong men; the kind of men that she never wanted attention from and could do without.

Princess knew to never go home the same way twice. Ginger warned her that some men would become obsessed with her. She told her about the many times that she had men that followed her home before. She taught Princess how to be street smart and how to protect herself and her daughter. Ginger also taught her the tricks of the trade; grooming her even more as she got more and more famous. Her name was everywhere. Anytime an entertainer or an athlete came into town, they requested her. Her name was in rap lyrics, she was in videos; Princess was everywhere.

After about three years of working at the club, and renting an apartment, Princess had saved enough money to put a hefty down payment on her own home; a quaint little three-bedroom home, tucked far enough away from the club and that lifestyle as possible. She wanted to live in a quiet, suburban neighborhood; somewhere that reminded her of home. She wanted to give Nylah the best life she could possibly have, even putting her in a private school. Unfortunately, the one person that Ginger couldn't protect Princess from was Rick.

After about two years of Princess working at the club, Ginger saw the look in Rick's eyes when he would watch Princess dance. She knew that he was starting to fall for her, but Rick wasn't the type of man that you said "no" to and if Rick wanted Princess, he wouldn't take "no" for an answer. Not much frightened Ginger, but Ginger knew the type of man that Rick was. Rick held all the cards; including Ginger's. Yes, she and Rick were business partners, but Rick had the finances to fund the whole thing and if she tried to stop him, she and Princess would be out the door and she had worked too hard to get to where she was to lose it all for Princess or anyone; no matter how much she cared for them.

Rick started showering Princess with expensive gifts, that she would try to reject, but knew that she didn't want to make him angry because she needed the job. She was now finishing up at the community college, working her way towards a Bachelor of Science degree (Ginger helped her get her GED) and wanted to become an engineer. She only had two more years to go, and thought *if I could just play the role for two more years, I could leave this job and never look back*, but she didn't quite make it that long.

It was in the dead of winter; the club was packed. Everybody was celebrating Christmas and Rick had some real heavy hitters in the club that night. The bottles were flowing, all the dancers were there, and Princess was in the VIP lounge, as usual. She was especially requested by one of the entertainers performing at the club that night. One of the guys in the VIP section took Princess to the back for a private dance. Rick watched her as she led the guy back to the room.

Rick had been drinking incessantly, had snorted a few lines of cocaine, and became enraged with jealousy. It's not as though she had never given a private dance before, but it was something different about this night. That coupled with the alcohol he had ingested and cocaine he snorted, Rick was out of his mind.

Ginger saw Rick head to the room and she became terrified. She had seen that look before and knew what he was capable of. She tried intercepting him, but he just tossed her to the side like a rag doll. He was way too strong and way too high for Ginger to stop him, so she ran and grabbed one of the bouncers to try to help her.

When Rick got to the room, he snatched Princess off the guy's lap. The guy jumped up shouting "Hey, I paid a lot of money for this dance and she's just getting started!" Rick punched him in his stomach, doubling him over with pain and threw Princess over his shoulder, as she was kicking and screaming. One of the bouncers grabbed Rick, and Princess promptly tried to get away, but he grabbed her by her hair, and drug her out the back door.

Ginger was afraid to call the cops because she didn't want to lose her business; however, other onlookers followed them out; a few of them had their phones out. Some were calling the cops, others were recording the whole scene in fear. No one jumped in to save her as he continually beat and kicked her while screaming obscenities at her and spitting on her; telling her that she was done and that he was going to mess her face up so that no one would ever want to look at her again.

Rick finally stopped, after she was no longer fighting back, and he heard sirens. Her eyes were swollen shut, her face was bloody, and she was coughing up blood. He left her there in the alley, alone. Everyone was running and screaming back through the club and started clearing out the front door. No one wanted to be in his path and no one was trying to be a witness for the cops to interrogate. Princess just lay there; alone and unable to move. She tried to crawl to get to the front, where she now heard the cop cars pulling up, but she could barely breathe. It felt as though her ribs were fractured, puncturing her lungs.

Suddenly, out of nowhere, appeared this figure in all black. Princess was terrified that it might be someone Rick had sent to clean up his mess and get rid of her (he had been known to do that), but instead, he leaned down and whispered in her ear "You're going to be ok. You are safe now. We're going to make sure that you get to the hospital and that no one will ever harm you again". She couldn't see his face, because her eyes were so swollen. All she could see was his silhouette.

He motioned for the ambulance to come to the alley where they were. As they were pulling in, the dark shadow disappeared into the night. Barely breathing and gasping for breath Princess managed to inquire about the whereabouts of the man that helped her.

"There was no man, ma'am. We saw no one when we pulled up. Who did this to you?" Afraid for her life, she whispered "I don't know. I didn't see his face". She just wanted to get out of there and fast.

The Police showed up to try to get statements from those that were left, but no one would talk. Rick held a lot of weight in that town. Everyone was afraid for their lives, even those that recorded the attack "live" quickly removed them that night, in fear of Rick's henchmen finding out who they were and where they lived.

The next morning, Princess was looking through her things, trying to find her phone. She needed to call

Nylah's babysitter to let her know where she was and to ask her if she could keep her for a couple of days, until she got out of the hospital. While looking for her phone, she ran across something that she had never seen before. She could barely make out what appeared to be a business card that read: **101 Front St NW, Baltimore, January 3, 2019, 6:00 PM.**

5 THE SELFIE QUEEN

Jacqui was ten years old when her father left. His leaving changed her life forever. It wasn't long after her father left, that her mother, Julie, started having men come in and out of her life, like a revolving door. Julie never seemed to pay much attention to Jacqui anymore. She put all her time and attention into the men that were in and out of her life. Jacqui resented Julie for that and felt like she was an orphan; abandoned and left to raise herself. She had no father, and felt as though she had no mother, either.

Julie worked hard all day, waitressing at the diner on the corner, but she played even harder at night. She was so self-absorbed that she had no idea what Jacqui was doing behind closed doors. The truth of the matter is that Julie was empty, too. With each man that left, it was like they took a piece of Julie with them. Like Julie, Jacqui looked to men to fill the void that was in her heart, when Jacqui's father left, but it only created an even greater void. This was the example of love and relationships that Jacqui had growing up.

Jacqui had a best friend, Justice, which she had known since she was eleven years old. They met around the same time that Jacqui's father left. Jacqui remembered as clear as day when Justice walked into the classroom, a new student from California, looking just as belligerent and rebellious as Jacqui. Her brunette edgy bob, had streaks of electric blue and hot pink all through it. Her shorts were way too short, and her shirt was way too tight, and at the age of eleven, she was already more physically developed than any girl Jacqui had ever seen.

Jacqui and Justice went through everything together; every phase, which included those awkward preteen years where they both had pimples and braces, up until they ditched the braces, pimples, and became buxom beauties. They were pretty much all they had. When they were going through their "ugly duckling" phase, they were bullied practically every day. They didn't have the best clothes, they knew nothing about make-up, and had poor hygiene because their mothers had no time for them to teach them how to take care of themselves and be ladies. Jacqui's mother was just too into herself, and Justice's mom worked three jobs because she was newly divorced and had no help taking care of Justice. All the two girls wanted was some attention, and boy did they get it.

By the time the girls were seventeen, they were a force to be reckoned with, when it came to the guys. They had the boys at their beckon call. They knew just what to do to get their attention, and social media was the gateway.

One day, Jacqui had gotten a direct message from one of the guys on the football team. It was the first time any guy, that every girl wanted, paid attention to her. He told her how much he liked her pictures on Instapic and asked if she would send him a private one that was a little more revealing. Thrilled that he was showing her any attention, Jacqui sent him a picture of her with just a bra and panties on.

In the picture, Jacqui was biting her bottom lip, her hair was wet, like she had just showered, showing her natural curls, and one of her bra straps was hanging off her shoulder. She was sitting with one knee up, so that you could see between her legs. Although she had on panties, she made sure that her pose would cause the guys to be aroused. She realized the more revealing her pictures were, the more "likes" and attention she would get. She liked the attention and became quite popular on Instapic. She figured that this could potentially jumpstart her career in the modeling and entertainment business and become the big star that she was always meant to be.

After a while, Jacqui and Justice grew weary of the "immature little boys" that were around their neighborhood. They had champagne taste and had to deal with guys that only had the budget for juice boxes. They had big dreams and none of them included staying around their small, stifling neighborhood. They wanted to be stars; Jacqui an actress and Justice a rock star and knew that they would never be discovered there.

Ever since Jacqui was a little girl, she always dreamed that she would see her name in lights; an Oscar award winning actress. She would write plays and pretend that her stuffed animals were her supporting cast in her stories as she always had the lead role.

Jacqui thought she had struck gold when one of her pictures caught the attention of a guy named Josh, that lived in Los Angeles. Josh told them that he worked for his uncle who was one of the biggest agents in Hollywood and if they were ever going to make it big, they couldn't do it in Maryland. He told them that they had to move out to Los Angeles where the real stars were.

Jacqui told Josh how it had always been her dream to live in Los Angeles, but how could she afford it, she would ask him. So, he promised her that once she got out to Los Angeles, he would make sure she had her own place, someone that could do professional headshots and a portfolio for her and set her up with a big named agent. Since Jacqui had been talking to Josh for months, now, and he seemed to be legit (Justice checked his credentials), Jacqui agreed to go out there to at least see what would happen. There was no way that Justice was allowing her to go alone and figured *What do we have to lose?* and decided to go with her.

After plotting out how they would get away, they waited for the right moment to execute their plan. At around 3 AM, early one Saturday morning, like clockwork, Justice's mother came home from work, went straight to her bedroom, and crashed. Justice went through her purse and took all the money she had in her wallet, which amounted to about $250. She knew that her mom worked at the bar on the weekends, waitressing, and always made at least $200 in tips every night. Bags already packed, she slung it over her shoulder, placed a note on the kitchen table, and crept out the back door, making sure she made no sounds as not to awaken her mother.

Jacqui waited until her mother was completely drunk, which also happened like clockwork, and came stumbling through the doorway. She had with her, some big, tall, dark haired, scruffy bearded man she picked up from the bar that night. Jacqui asked her if she could have some money to go out with Justice to the movies. Her mother, smelling like a brewery and like she had smoked eighteen packs of cigarettes (although she didn't smoke), waved Jacqui towards her purse and continued to stagger towards her bedroom door, slobbing down her burly stranger.

When Jacqui reached into her mother's purse, all she found was a bunch of receipts, but no cash. Frustrated, she threw the wallet down, until she remembered that she knew her mother's PIN number to her debit card. Figuring that by the time she'd awaken and realized her card was missing, Jacqui would be long gone, she snatched the card, grabbed her bag, and ran out the door.

Justice was standing in the cold brisk air, teeth chattering, and freezing her butt off, when Jacqui finally showed up to their meet up place; the bus stop. "What the hell took you so long?"

Jacqui held up her hand to Justice with her eyes rolled up into her head and cut her off. "I had to wait for my mother to get home, so I could get the money" she said, obviously annoyed.

"Well, did you?" asked Justice.

"Yeah. I had to stop by the ATM to get money from her debit card because she had no cash" she replied while pulling the money out of the wallet. "How much were you able to get from your mom?"

"I was only able to get $250. What about you?" Justice eagerly anticipating Jacqui's response, hoping it was much more than she could scrounge up.

With a panicked, yet hopeful look on her face, Jacqui gave the money to Justice. "I was able to get about $400 out of mom's account"

"Holy crap! How'd she manage to have that much?" cried Justice with excitement. "Never mind. It doesn't matter how" she said as she took out $160 and stuffed the rest of the money into her wallet. "I'm just glad you got it!"

The girls walked over to the counter at the bus terminal and bought two one-way tickets for a straight trip from Baltimore to North Carolina for $75 each, which only left them with the $500. They knew that they had to budget their money well, or they would either not make it to Los Angeles, or would have to find ways to make more money, quickly.

As the bus left the terminal, the girls realized how exhausted they were and before long, Justice's head was pressed up against the window, while Jacqui's head rested on Justice's shoulders. They stayed that way until the sun pierced brightly through the clouds, almost blinding Justice, and the bus driver made the announcement over the speaker that they had to stop for gas. He continued to inform them that everyone had to get all their belongings off the bus and take them with them until he was finished getting the gas.

Everyone started gathering their belongings and slowly, one by one, getting off the bus. The girls checked the purses that they had wrapped around their hands and positioned in the front of their bodies to make sure no one would try to steal them while they slept. Everything was still in place, which was a huge relief. As Jacqui pulled her phone out of her purse, she saw that she had about ten missed calls from her mother all with voicemail messages of her mother cussing her out for taking her ATM card; no concern for her well-being at all. Jacqui wasn't surprised, though. She always felt like she was in her mom's way and kept her from living the life she wanted to live.

Justice, on the other hand, was disappointed that her mother, Belinda, didn't even notice that she was gone. She barely saw her mother and while she understood why her mother worked so hard, Justice still resented Belinda's choice of men that caused them to be in this situation in the first place. Justice's father had been locked up for as long as she could remember. She never asked about why he was locked up and she never saw him. All her mom told her was that he was in jail and wouldn't be getting out for at least twenty years.

Belinda's husband, Jim, was no better. Jim was into drugs and all sorts of illegal affairs. He would come home drunk or high and would beat Belinda when she tried to protect Justice from being raped and molested by him; which he had been doing to her from the time that she was six years old until he was arrested when she was ten years old. When Jim was arrested and brought up on weapons and drug charges, Belinda saw that as her opportunity to get them as far away from him as possible. She filed for divorce and moved Justice across the country to Baltimore, where one of her best friends, Beth, lived. Beth was the one that helped them escape.

Jacqui decided to block her mother's number. She knew that she had taken all the money that she had in her account, out, anyway, so she ripped the card up and threw it away in Baltimore. She didn't want anyone to be able to track where they were going. The last place that they could trace them to was North Carolina, and that's the way Jacqui wanted it.

Since it was one o'clock in the afternoon, and they hadn't eaten since the night before, they wanted to grab a quick bite to eat before getting on their next bus to Texas. It wasn't set to leave for another two hours, so they had time to kill. They found a Mr. D's across the street, which worked out perfectly for their budget. They could get two items a piece on the dollar menu and get soda out of the soda machine for fifty cents.

With the first bite of their burgers and fries, they closed their eyes and let out a sigh. It was like tasting heaven to them. They took their time eating because they didn't know how long it would be before they'd be able to eat again.

Three o'clock came quickly, which they were happy about. All they wanted to do was get off their feet. Once they got settled into their seats, they looked over and noticed a little boy staring at them from across the aisle. He had dirty blonde hair cut in the shape of a bowl and had the prettiest aqua blue eyes they had ever seen. He was a handsome little fella; couldn't have been more than three or four years old. His name was Brian. They knew that because they kept hearing his mother call his name frequently. He was a rather busy little boy.

Every time they went to sleep and woke up, Brian was staring at them. It was like he never slept and was hopped up on sugar or something. For some reason, Jacqui was drawn to this little boy. It almost felt like they were kindred spirits. For hours, she entertained him, keeping him busy, which his mother was thrilled about. It gave her a break.

By the time they got to Texas, they were so over being on the bus. Their young, eighteen-year-old bodies felt like they had just been beaten up. All they wanted to do was stretch out somewhere. They checked their funds to see if they had enough to just get a room to rest for the night, before venturing further west to Los Angeles. Jacqui looked at the prices for the bus to Las Vegas and then for the price of the tickets to Los Angeles. Realizing they wouldn't have enough to make it all the way, Justice decided that they had to come up with a plan B to make some extra cash, and quick!

The girls decided that if they could at least make it to Vegas, there were numerous ways in which they could make some fast cash. They had enough for a room for the night and felt like if they could just make an extra two-hundred dollars in some way, they could get the rest of the way. "Hey! Maybe we could call Josh and he could just give us a loan until we get there and get jobs to pay him back?" Jacqui asked. "Do you think he would?"

"Probably" Justice responded, shrugging her shoulders in a nonchalant manner. "He would do anything you ask him to do, Jacqui. I know he is definitely feeling YOU!" she said, rolling her eyes. Justice had a bad feeling about the guy, although she would never let Jacqui know that. Jacqui seemed to think she knew him well enough to go out to LA and Justice was not about to let her go alone. Jacqui wasn't as street savvy as she was.

Jacqui grabbed her phone and called him. "Hello?" he said, answering her call.

"Hey Josh! How are you?" she said with the widest smile; feeling butterflies at just the sound of his voice.

"I'm good. I'm good. Are you guys out here yet?" he asked with excitement in his voice.

"No. Not yet. We're in Texas. We're running low on cash and was wondering if …." She stopped and took in a breath, feeling apprehensive about what she was about to ask. "…perhaps you had maybe like two hundred dollars you could wire us, just until we got there and got jobs to pay you back?" as the phone went silent for a second, she continued "We will pay you back with our first paycheck. We promise!" Jacqui begged with the pouty sexy voice that he could never seem to say no to.

"Of course. I'll Western Union it to you. You know I'll do anything for you, Jacqui" he said with that silky tone of his.

"You are so sweet", she cooed in his ear, while Justice motioned like she was about to vomit, sticking her finger in her mouth, rolling her eyes. She knew Jacqui had him wrapped around her finger just like she had all the other guys that fell for her; at least she thought she did. As soon as she got off the phone, they ran to the closest motel, booked a room, and asked where the nearest Western Union was, so when he texted them the information, they wouldn't have to waste much time getting there. Luckily, it was right across the street at the local grocery store and so was a Burger Paradise.

The girls, again, were starving! They wanted to wait until they heard from Josh, first, so they could make one trip across that busy highway, so they just hung out in their room, took showers, and changed their clothes. It felt so good to be clean and in some fresh clothes again. The weather was much warmer in Texas, so they changed into some cooler clothes. Justice had on a pair of skimpy cut-off jean shorts, and a white fitted tank top, and hot pink track shoes. Jacqui was equally scantily clad, with black bootie shorts, a fitted tee and a pair of black high-top biker boots. They always loved to show off their curves.

Within the hour, Josh had texted them the information for the money transfer, so they grabbed their jackets, purses, and room key, and ran out the door. They went to the grocery store and bought a couple of snacks for the bus ride for the next day, got the money, and then went to Burger Paradise, where they got two kids meals. Even though Josh sent them money, they still wanted to be frugal with it. They didn't know how long it would take them to get jobs when they got there, or when they would get their first paycheck.

When they arrived back to their room, they tore the bags open and started munching on those burgers and fries like they were ravenous wolves! The food was so good to them, but they couldn't wait to get to LA to go to all the fabulous restaurants that Josh had promised to take them. Neither of them had ever gone to a fancy restaurant. For them, going out to dinner meant Joe's Diner in their hometown. Their mothers never had the money or the time to take them anywhere else.

Finally, down for the night, feeling as though they were laying in a bed of clouds, the girls drifted off to sleep. In the middle of the night, Justice abruptly woke up screaming. It scared Jacqui so bad that she fell out of the bed screaming, herself. "Justice, what is going on?!"

"I'm sorry. I must've had a nightmare, but it seemed so real", Justice said, still trembling from the dream. She continued. "We were in this dark, gloomy basement or cellar, and we were chained to a bar that was attached to the floor. We weren't the only ones there. There were several other girls" she said, sitting up slowly in the bad, as she wiped her eyes trying to collect herself. "I couldn't see their faces and I couldn't tell how many, but it just felt so real". The more she spoke, the more intense the trembling in her entire body became.

"It was just a bad dream, Justice. Look, we're fine. It's just you and me" Jacqui said as she tried to soothe and console her friend. Jacqui had never seen Justice so afraid. *Justice isn't afraid of anything, so for her to be acting like this, it must be bad,* Jacqui thought to herself. "We have each other's backs", she continued to say to Justice trying to ease her mind. "If we're together, nothing bad will happen to either of us" she said, reassuringly.

Although it made Jacqui a bit nervous, she would never tell Justice that. They knew that going somewhere they had never been before, trusting a guy they had never met before, was taking a huge risk, but Jacqui felt it was a risk they had to take. They knew they would never reach their dreams in their small town. Besides, no one ever made it big without taking risks.

Josh told the girls to call him when they got to Las Vegas. He said that he had to go to Vegas for a meeting and may be there when they arrived, and if that was the case, the girls could just head back to LA with him. *That would be wonderful,* Jacqui thought to herself.

The girls were riding on the bus through what seemed to be a black hole for hours. It seemed like no life existed anywhere. They were in the middle of the desert. All they knew is that it was hot, and they couldn't wait to get to Las Vegas. They had never been anywhere outside of their small town, and the excitement was starting to take over.

Suddenly, out of the blackness, there seemed to be nothing but lights that appeared everywhere. They had never seen so much light in one place before. It just looked like a million stars shining in one spot. As they drove closer, they were amazed at all the massive duplicates of the Brooklyn Bridge and the Statue of Liberty at New York, New York; the opulence of the fountains at the Bellagio; the replica of the Eiffel Tower at Paris, Paris; and the beautiful lake and Gondolas that flowed out of the Venetian.

The girls were in awe. Jacqui quickly texted Josh to let him know that they were in Las Vegas, and he quickly responded and said that he was still there and would send a car to meet them at the bus station. "A car to pick us up?!" Jacqui screamed with exhilaration. Although Jacqui was super amped up, Justice still seemed to be a little uneasy. She just could not shake that dream.

"Why can't he just come get us? Why does he have to send a car?" she questioned with a disgruntled tone in her voice and look on her face. "Something just doesn't feel right about this".

Jacqui started to get anxious because Justice was scaring her, but not wanting Justice to know, Jacqui curtly stated, "Justice, he can't. He's in a meeting". As Jacqui snatched her bags out of the luggage compartment of the bus, she continued "He's a big-time manager. He doesn't have time to babysit us. We must act like adults, now. He can't just drop what he's doing. It'll be fine. It's Josh. He wouldn't let anything happen to us".

As the bus pulled into the terminal, they saw a man, with a menacing face, dressed in all black, with the darkest shades they had ever seen. *Shades at night? What for?* thought Justice to herself before shrugging it off. *Must be a Hollywood thing.* The man was holding a sign with their names on it. Jacqui, again, jumped up and down, brimming with enthusiasm. While she felt as though they had "arrived", Justice felt the complete opposite. Still thinking about that nightmare, she became even more increasingly apprehensive.

The limousine was everything Jacqui imagined it would be and more. They noticed a bottle of champagne chilling and two glasses with a note that said "Turn up! You're about to embark upon the journey of a lifetime". Jacqui was so excited, so Justice pretended to be for the sake of her friend. She didn't want to bring Jacqui down with her skepticism. *Besides, maybe this was exactly what Jacqui thought it would be and I'm just jaded because of my past*, she thought. They had never had any champagne. The only alcohol that they had ever had was wine coolers that they stole from Jacqui's mom.

As they started guzzling down the champagne, they started feeling a little strange. They looked at each other and their faces seemed disfigured and blurry. They thought the car was spinning in circles and everything seemed to be going in slow motion. By the time they started to realize this wasn't just from being drunk, it was too late.

When the girls finally woke up, Justice let out a blood curdling scream; it was just like her nightmare. There they were, in a dark room, which appeared to be a basement or dungeon of some sorts. They were chained to a pipe that was bolted to the cement floor. They tried to see what was going on in the room from the slither of light that was coming from a tiny window near the ceiling.

The pungent stench of urine, feces, and garbage in the room made Justice vomit. From what they could tell, this wasn't the first time someone had been down there. Right beside them were other sets of handcuffs attached to the bar, tin plates with rotten food on it, and remnants of women's clothing scattered around.

"We've been set up by that loser, Josh!" Justice yelled at Jacqui. "I knew we never should have trusted him". Just as Jacqui was about to respond, they heard footsteps coming and voices of men that weren't speaking in any language that the girls had ever heard. As the men finally reached the girls, Jacqui and Justice tried to make out their faces, but could only see their silhouettes.

One man grabbed Jacqui and put a dingy cloth over her mouth. Her body went limp. 'Oh my God, Jacqui, wake up!! What have you done to her?" Justice yelled, sobbing, kicking, and trying her best to break free. Two men came in the room and dragged Jacqui out. As Justice was screaming, one man came behind her and covered her mouth with the same dirty cloth and out she went; just like Jacqui. This time when they woke up, things were quite different.

Jacqui started coming to and quickly realized Justice was no longer with her. As she looked around, she saw luxurious gold and purple drapery surrounding these enormous French doors that led out to a balcony. The view was magnificent. *Where am I?* she thought to herself. As she tried to collect her thoughts, she began freaking out about Justice; wondering where she was, what they had done to her, and was she still alive? As she laid on the bed, she ran her hands across her stomach, and noticed that she was completely topless. She sat up, still groggy from whatever they drugged her with, trying to cover her exposed breasts with her hands. As she pulled back the black satiny sheets that were draped across her legs, she was utterly mortified to discover that she was completely naked.

Jacqui, then, jumped up off the bed in hysterics. *Oh, my God! Why am I naked?* she thought, as she started to wonder how long she had been naked and what had they done to her. On the bed beside her was a red, satin teddy that laced up in the front and was cut out where the breasts belonged, with black fishnet thigh highs, a garter belt, and 6-inch black platform heels. *Did I have that on or are they going to put it on me?* she wondered. Still scared out of her mind, she ran to the bathroom that was attached to the room, threw her head in the toilet and violently began to vomit. Just the thought that someone had sex with her without her consent, made her sick to her stomach.

As she slowly pulled herself up off the floor, Jacqui caught a glimpse of herself in the mirror. She had on heavy makeup, with ruby red lipstick and smoky eyes. She didn't even look like herself. *How long was I out?* She thought to herself. *How did I not feel any of this going on?* She felt like such a naïve, little, child for trusting Josh. She hoped that Justice was wrong about him and his involvement in all of this. She could only hope that she wasn't that stupid for believing in him and getting her best friend involved in all of this, too.

Just as she was getting herself together and trying to figure out how she was going to get out of there and look for Justice, an older balding, portly man appeared in the doorway. He was wearing this tacky shiny gray suit, white spread collar shirt that was opened, showing his grizzly chest hair that made her want to vomit all over again, and white patent leather penny loafers. He had a hand full of gold rings, and a thick gold chain that was protruding through his thick, beady looking, salt and pepper chest hair. He was looking at her like she was a piece of meat he was about to devour.

"What do you want?" Jacqui asked as she started slowly backing away from him, awkwardly trying to cover up her body. As if he couldn't get any worse, he smiled, showing off a big ol' gold tooth. He started talking, but she couldn't understand a thing that he was saying. He was speaking in what appeared to be the same foreign language that the other guys were speaking. He walked closer before lunging at her.

Jacqui started to scream "Get away from me, you creep and where is Justice?", but it didn't seem to bother him or stop him one bit. She was backed into a corner and had nowhere to go. She looked for something to hit him with, but there was nothing.

As the man grabbed her, she kneed him in the groin, pushed him out of the way, and ran to the door, but when she opened it, there was this tall, robust, scary looking bodyguard that looked like he was about seven feet tall, weighing about three hundred pounds, that picked her up and threw her back in the room, onto the bed. He had a needle in his hand and as he straddled Jacqui on the bed and she couldn't move, he stuck her arm with the needle.

Jacqui wasn't completely out of it, as the needle did not go all the way into her arm because she was fighting so much. Unfortunately, she was coherent enough to know what was going on, she just had no strength to fight back. As the old, fat man started taking his clothes off, the bodyguard walked out. After he took off his clothes, the man started to slither towards Jacqui's naked body, and she felt completely helpless. She knew what was about to happen.

Just as he was about to climb on top of her, there was a loud noise, and he jumped up. He threw a robe on and started yelling, she guessed, for his bodyguard. *I must find a way to get out of here and go find Justice*, Jacqui thought to herself. She tried to muster up as much strength as she could to stand up. She looked everywhere for her own clothes or at least for some clothes that would cover her exposed body. She found a big t-shirt and some shorts in one of the dresser drawers in the room. She didn't care if she had to run around with bare feet, she had to get out of there.

Although everything was blurry, and she saw things in doubles, Jacqui was determined to get out and find Justice. Stumbling all over the place, she managed to put the clothes on, but just as she opened the door, she ran right into one of the bodyguards. He was about to pick her up and throw her back into the room, when she heard Justice's voice cry out to her "Jacqui!!". She turned and saw Justice dressed up in clothes like the ones that were laying on the bed beside her, but she was with a man that was dragging her outside and into a black SUV.

Jacqui was about to run out the door after her and suddenly felt a thump on the back of her head. She almost blacked out again but saw a man with a black ski mask dressed in all camouflage, hit the bodyguard on the head from behind with a crowbar and grabbed Jacqui and placed her on the step out of harm's way. *Who was he and what was* **he** *about to do with her*, she thought to herself? The masked man ran over and started fighting with the bodyguard as he was holding the back of his head and started to charge after the masked man.

At first, the bodyguard was getting the best of him, but out of nowhere, suddenly, he gained what seemed like superhero strength and just picked up the bodyguard and threw him into the wall. The bodyguard hit his head on one of the end tables that was in the hallway and was knocked out cold. He grabbed Jacqui, threw her over his shoulder, and ran around the corner, in front of the garage.

When they got to the garage, there was a black SUV of some sort, waiting for them. Although Jacqui was somewhat apprehensive about getting in the truck, (the last time they got in a vehicle they ended up there) she figured this guy just risked his life to rescue her, and what other options did she have? She had no idea where she was.

Although it was dark, Jacqui could tell it didn't even look like she was in the United States anymore, from the looks of the houses in the surrounding area. They rode in the SUV, for what seemed to be hours. She was now completely coherent.

As she leaned against the window, looking out, Jacqui noticed that there were palm trees everywhere, but not the lush looking ones that she had seen in pictures. There were these little houses that looked like rundown shacks. The roads had no pavement or lines. The few people that were out at that time of night had very dark, tan skin. The whole community seemed to look like it was impoverished. Most of them rode bikes or were on foot. Jacqui had no clue where they were or how they got there, but she knew they were a long way from home.

Exhausted from everything that had taken place, along with the fact that she still had drugs in her system and no clue as to where her best friend was, she passed out from exhaustion. When the truck finally stopped, she was at some old haunted looking shack. It was dirty looking, delipidated and somewhat hidden behind a bunch of trees.

"Oh no!" Jacqui cried out loud, "What are we doing here?" Immediately attempting to break free from the seatbelt that was wrapped around her waist, forgetting where she was. "I just want to find my friend and go home" she sobbed, frustrated that she couldn't get the seatbelt off fast enough.

Jacqui tried to calm down, but all she could do was think about her friend and everything that they had just gone through. Justice was the one that could usually sense when something was off, and she did. She kept saying that this whole trip was a bad idea, but she didn't want Jacqui to go alone. Even though she felt uneasy and wasn't as discerning as Justice was, she knew that these people were here to help her. At least she prayed that they were.

The passenger that was in the front, got out of the SUV. Jacqui couldn't see any of their faces. They all wore the same black masks and camouflage as the guy that rescued her; however, Jacqui realized from their stature that the passenger was a woman. When the passenger returned to the car, she handed Jacqui some toiletries, and clean clothes. "These are for you to take quick shower, and to change clothes. There's a plane waiting for us on airstrip to take you back to de states. Hurry! We don't have much time. They will be looking for us" she said hurriedly in broken English.

"Wait! What about Justice?" she cried out after her, as the woman quickly spun around to leave. The woman stopped, turned back towards Jacqui, looking at her with a solemn look on her face.

"I don't know where you friend is. She could be anywhere now" resting an empathetic hand on Jacqui's shoulder. "I explain more, later, but if you don't do what I ask you to do now, we may all end up dead and never know what happen to your friend" the woman said slightly pushing her forward.

So, Jacqui did as she was told and quickly took a shower and changed her clothes in the tiny house that looked like it was just big enough to be an efficiency apartment back home. Everything was in one room; kitchen, living room, and bedroom all in one. Honestly, the way it looked on the outside, she was shocked that it even had running water. There were mats on the wooden floor, where it looked as if people slept and they had IV poles beside the beds and medical supplies such as bandages, gauze, and slings.

Jacqui looked to the right of her, where she saw two other girls; one black and one that looked Asian, that looked about her same age or younger. They had just taken showers and gotten dressed. They looked scared out of their minds, like they had been through way more than Jacqui had just escaped from. The girls didn't ask any questions, although Jacqui had a million going through her mind that she wanted to ask. She could tell that this was some type of refuge for people.

All the girls were rushed back out to the black SUV that had brought Jacqui there, but when they walked out, they were a little startled to see men standing by the door with machine guns. These guys were menacing, which caused the girls to stop apprehensively before being encouraged to continue. Although they were startled at first and the men did look extremely intimidating, somehow, they knew that they were safe.

As the girls and the masked individuals headed to the airstrip, the truck was eerily silent. No one spoke; not even the driver and passenger to one another. Jacqui could tell that this was something they did often. They seemed very organized and moved with precision and swiftness. It caused her to consider how many girls had gone through what they had just gone through or worse, and if these girls that were with her had suffered the same or worse fate as she did. She shuddered at the thought of it. Her thoughts again shifted to her best friend. She didn't even want to imagine where Justice was or what she was going through.

Finally reaching the airstrip, they were greeted by a woman and a man that also had on the masks and camouflage. *This must be their uniform, but who are they*, Jacqui pondered in her mind. The girls were told to go to the airplane and that the airplane was going to take them back to the states. They further informed them that once they got back to the states, their families would be waiting for them when they landed. *How did they know who we are or where we came from, not to mention knowing how to contact our families*, she wondered in amazement? She had never talked to them before, nor had she or Justice revealed any of their information to anyone but Josh.

On the plane, Jacqui began to think of one of the last conversations she had with Justice. "Justice, do you think Josh was even involved in any of this? What if he was a victim too? If so, where is he and do you think he's hurt?" Jacqui whispered as they sat handcuffed to the pole in the basement.

Having no doubt in her mind, Justice responded "Get your head out of the clouds, Jacqui. Josh had everything to do with what happened to us, like I said, and he's probably been doing this to girls for a long time. Your boyfriend's a freakin' scam artist and he reeled us in, hook line, and sinker" she yelled grimacing in disbelief at Jacqui's naivete.

"I'm sure there was a big payday in it for him" she said as she scowled, turning away in sheer frustration. Justice wanted revenge in the worst way and had made up in her mind that she was going to get it, as soon as she got out of there; *but I don't even know if she ever made it out alive*, Jacqui cringed, horrified at the thought. She began to panic and started having anxiety when she began to think *What am I going to tell her mother?* She started hyperventilating and freaking out on the plane, so they restrained her and gave her a mild sedative to calm her and help her sleep.

The flight was so long that all the girls had fallen asleep, but halfway through, they were awakened with a boxed lunch. There was a turkey and cheese sandwich, a bag of chips, apple slices, and a juice box. Ridiculously starving, the girls scarfed down the food within minutes. It tasted like a steak dinner to them. They hadn't eaten in what seemed like weeks, and who knows, maybe months for the other girls, although it had only been two days for

Jacqui. Shortly after they ate, the girls fell back to sleep with Jacqui laying against the window. She imagined it was Justice's arm she was leaning on.

Although they were the same age, Justice had a little more common sense and streets smarts than Jacqui and had always felt like she had to protect her. Justice was very nurturing and had a mothering presence about her. *I must find her*, Jacqui thought to herself. Before Jacqui had fallen back to sleep, she put her hand in her pocket to keep her hands warm, and she found a card in it. She pulled the card out and it read: **101 Front St NW, Baltimore, January 3, 2019, 6:00 PM.** *What is this?* she thought to herself. *Maybe this is where I'll be able to find Justice. Maybe this is where she'll meet me.*

6 THE REBELLIOUS RAPPER

"He's crashing! I need the crash cart stat! We're losing him! We're losing him!" screamed the nurses at Mercy Medical Hospital as they rushed the gurney down the hallway. There he was, Matteo Matthews, AKA "Kilo" the hottest new rapper around; had the world at his feet. All the girls wanted him, and all the fellas wanted to be like him and he's lying on a gurney about to die. As he started fading away, he started thinking to himself *Is this how my life is going to end?* And before you knew it, his eyes rolled in the back of his head and he started to flat line. How far he had fallen from the shy little well-mannered church boy from Baltimore County, Maryland that he used to be.

Matteo's father, John Matthews, Jr., was African American and his mother, Alicia Lopez, was Puerto Rican. He didn't know much about his Puerto Rican side because he was raised by his paternal grandparents. His grandfather, John Mathews, Sr. or Pop-Pop John as Matteo called him, was a Pastor of one of the oldest and most prestigious African American churches in the region, started by Matteo's great-great grandfather John-Henry Matthews. Matteo heard many stories about how John-Henry

Matthews was a freed slave; with a strong faith in God. John-Henry's first-born son, Matteo's great grandfather Alexander Matthews, promised his father that they would always keep God at the center of their family and never allow anyone to tear down the church that he built with his bare hands.

Of course, back then, the church sat on an acre of dusty flat land that was acquired by John-Henry from his slave owners because they couldn't grow anything on it. It was useless to them, but it was all John-Henry needed. Day and night, he slaved away putting hammer to nail to build this tiny little white shack with an aluminum roof, and hard wooden benches, with only about ten freed slaves and their families that attended. From the time that the doors opened on that little shack of a church, until the time it had become a palatial Pentecostal sanctuary sitting on seven acres of land right in the middle of the inner city of Baltimore, their family had taken great pride in it. With over six thousand active members, it had become a staple in the community. It was their family's legacy.

Matteo was being groomed by his Pop-Pop John to take over the church when he was ready to retire, but Matteo did not want to be a preacher and had no intentions on becoming the pastor of their family's church. He believed in God but preaching and pastoring was a calling that he did not want, nor did he feel like he had. He resented his father because he felt that his father and mother chose drugs over him, and now the burden of the church and carrying on the family's legacy seemed his responsibility when it should have been his father's.

Matteo could barely remember his father, John, Jr. or his mother, and his grandparents wouldn't even talk to him about them. Every time Matteo would ask questions about his father, all they would say was that he chose the fast life and drugs over God, and that Matteo was better off without them being in his life. He couldn't understand how they could say such things. *Yes, he may have made mistakes and made wrong choices, but at the end of the day, he was still their son. How could they call themselves Christians and how could they preach about forgiveness, when they harbored so much anger and unforgiveness in their hearts towards their own son?* Matteo often wondered. There were no pictures around of him; nothing. They acted as though he didn't exist anymore; well at least it seemed that way with Pop-Pop John.

Matteo could always tell that his grandmother, Gladys's heart still ached for her son whenever Matteo would ask questions, but it was like she wasn't allowed to express that out loud; especially not around her husband. Grandma Gladys would mention him every now and then, saying that Matteo was so much like him. She would have a weary smile on her face; looking into the distance. Rocking in her rocking chair she would say things in a soft, whispering voice, like "a mother never stops loving or longing for their children when they're lost" or "I pray for your father every day, that God would bring him back to Him even if he doesn't bring him back to us". To Pop-Pop John, however, John. Jr. was a disappointment to the family and disgraced their name.

Matteo grew up in church all his life. He wasn't allowed to listen to secular music, couldn't go to any school dances, he couldn't even go to the movies. His grandparents called those places "the devil's playground" and they wanted him to steer clear of it. When he was younger, he was frightened to even think about going to any of those places. He didn't know why the devil liked to play there, but he knew he didn't want to play with him. He used to ask his friends when they would tell them that they had been to the movies, why they had been playing with the devil. They would give him these baffled looks and just shake their heads, as they shooed him away or ignored him. At the age of five, he didn't know any better and neither did they.

By the time Matteo hit Middle School, however, he was aware of what his grandparents meant when they said it was the "devil's playground" and thoroughly aware of what he felt like he was missing. They thought that those places would tempt people to "sin". Little did they know, you can sin pretty much anywhere you go and where you went didn't have much to do with it. *Shoot, I see people sinning right in the church*, he thought to himself.

Matteo listened to enough sermons and read enough of his Bible throughout all the Bible studies, Vacation Bible School, and Sunday School lessons, to know that God looked at the intent of a person's heart. While sin was sin, he also knew there were other things that people held in on the inside that God didn't like, either; like unforgiveness. So, when they would have middle school dances, Matteo would lie and tell Grandma Gladys that he had to stay after school for tutoring. He knew she wouldn't get out of the car to check and would just pick him up.

Grandma believed everything Matteo said because he was her perfect little angel, and what she did know, she pretended not to, because she did not want John, Sr. to run him away, like he did John, Jr.

The middle school dances are where Matteo had his first experience with girls. He was always a handsome fella, with his smooth, buttery caramel skin and his silky black curls that swirled around on the top of his head. He had the deepest dimples that looked like coin slots when he smiled. He was a heartthrob and when he realized it, he used it to his advantage. He had girls doing his homework, bringing him lunch to school, and fighting over him. He just knew he was the man; especially after he got his first kiss from Brianna.

Brianna took Matteo behind the bleacher at a one of their school dances and just grabbed his head and pulled it close to hers, planting a big, juicy kiss on his lips. Matteo's face tuned so red, he looked like he was on fire! He couldn't describe how that kiss made him feel. All he knew was that it made him want to keep doing it. Brianna asked him if he wanted to be her boyfriend and he said yes; especially if it meant he could do THAT some more. He and Brianna dated off and on from 8th grade throughout high school.

By the time Matteo had gotten to high school, he didn't want to be the "church boy". He had started working after school and could buy his own clothes. That's when his real swag started to kick in. He had also realized that he had started to become a decent rapper. He had gotten introduced to rap when he was in Middle school.

His best friend at church, Brian, whose parents allowed him to listen to secular music, introduced him to it.

Brian liked to rap too, so they would go home from school and write raps and then when Matteo didn't have to work, they would go over to Brian's house and record their raps to see who had the hottest "bars". As much as Brian hated to admit it Matteo's was always the hottest. They started to upload some of their raps online and soon, they started having a strong following.

Matteo had the "it" factor. He had charisma, the looks, he was a prolific thinker, wise beyond his years, and everyone loved him; well everyone, that is, except those that hated on him for those very same qualities. There were those that wanted to be like him, but no matter how hard they tried, they just didn't have "it". Matteo knew it and sometimes, he allowed it to go to his head, but every now and then, he would get knocked down a couple of pegs to remind him that he hadn't "arrived" yet.

One day, Pop-Pop John realized he had a great burden on him to reach out to the youth in their community. He especially had a burden for the boys and young men. He could see the path that many of them had already taken and wanted to intercept those who were headed that way, so he enlisted the help of Matteo and his friends.

"I want to have a rally to get the neighborhood involved in reaching out to these kids on these corners. Many of them are your peers, Matteo. What can we do? What will draw their attention?" Pop-Pop John inquired.

Matteo chuckled under his breath a little before saying "Well, Pop-Pop, you're not going to get their attention with that old timey stuff y'all do down at the church. They're not trying to hear Deacon Jones and them singing those old negro spirituals that y'all pull out of the hymnals". Brian was snickering under his breath and Pop-Pop John looked over his glasses at him with a disapproving glare. Brian quickly stopped laughing and sat up straight in his chair. "You're going to have to do something that's a little more updated or you can forget it" Matteo continued.

"Like what?" asked Pop-Pop John sincerely interested in what his grandson had to say.

Matteo shifted his weight to his right side and looked at his grandfather like he was afraid to say what he really wanted to say because he had a feeling how his grandfather would respond." Do you really want my opinion Pop-Pop?" he asked.

"I wouldn't have asked if I didn't. Look, I know that you and I don't have the same idea of what real music is, but I feel like the good Lord wants me to reach out to these boys by any means necessary" he said as he stared intently at Matteo. "So, whatever ideas you have, if you think they'll work, let's hear them. I can take it for this one event".

Matteo realized that his grandfather was serious, so he said to him, "Well, Pop-Pop, hip hop is what my generation responds to. Rap. That's what speaks to us. That's what we feel best represents us. It's just poetry to music. We promise we won't say anything vulgar or anything that will disrespect the church or God". He clapped his hands tightly together as if he was praying and begging at the same time; which he was.

Matteo really wasn't as interested in his grandfather's intentions for this rally as he was his own. He knew something like that would be a great opportunity for him to showcase his skills in front of hundreds of people. One thing he knew for sure, was that anytime St. John's Missionary Baptist Church put on an event, people showed up!

"Fine, Matteo", Pop-Pop John reluctantly said. He knew in his mind that the boy was right. He just didn't know how the older "saints" would react to it. The last thing he needed was the board of trustees breathing down his back or walking out of the meeting when he presented it to them. They had a lot of clout as to how the church spent its finances.

"I'll get right on it" and that is exactly what Matteo did. Within a few days, the buzz about the event was all over social media. They had flyers that he and Brian had made by one of their friends. Brian even did a short commercial that he put on social media promoting the event. All the kids in school were talking about it, and once word got out on the street what was going down, people started paying attention to St. Johns in a different way.

There was so much excitement going on about the event and that Matteo would be the one of the performers, that as the time got closer, he started to get nervous. This thing had become way bigger than he anticipated. There were a lot of people coming to see him; not to mention that his grandfather and the church was depending on him and this event to be a success and weren't thrilled with the idea to begin with.

Although many people in the neighborhood had volunteered their services, and stores and businesses in the community donated food and drinks, St. Johns still had to put out a lot of money. *What if I choke? What if I forget my words? I'll be the laughing stock of the community.* He started to panic inside. *I heard that channel 13 news was going to be here and some of the local radio stations,* he thought to himself. *What if I fall flat on my face? I'll never be able to come back from that,* he thought as he paced back and forth and almost started to hyperventilate.

At that point, he knew there was no turning back. He had to suck it up and just make sure he prepared himself to lock this performance down. It was his big shot. He couldn't let his grandfather down, his friends that believed in him and supported him, nor could he let himself down.

The day of the big community rally arrived. There were people everywhere. Vendors were all set up, the food was on the grill, the sound engineers had come in and did sound check with him and some of the other groups that were performing. Some of the speakers walked around practicing their speeches. Things started to become very real for him. After two agonizing hours of waiting and pacing back and forth, praying, sweating, and feeling like he was almost about to black out at times, the moment had arrived. It was his turn to make his big debut. He walked up on stage, clothes were on point, looked good, and he was ready. Like a roaring lion he came from the back and just commanded the stage.

It was liked Matteo had morphed into this alter ego that was super confident and had no fear. He killed his performance! The crowd went crazy! They couldn't get enough of him. When he finished his song, he walked off the stage, but heard the people screaming his name. It was a sound he had only dreamed of hearing. *Are they screaming for me* he wondered in amazement, smiling from ear to ear? The emcee asked him if he had another song because the crowd was feeling him and wanted more. Luckily, he did because he had three songs prepared as back-ups, in the event of an emergency. Once again, he nailed it!

Little did Matteo know, there were some heavy hitters that were in the audience. Chris Thompson, one of the hottest hip hop producers in the business was one of them. Chris had very fond memories of St. Johns. When he was a kid, his grandmother would drag him and his brothers to Vacation Bible School during the summers when she babysat them while their mother worked. It was Pastor Matthews that kept them from being involved in the gangs in their neighborhood without even knowing it, so this event meant a great deal to him.

After Matteo came down off the stage, Chris was standing there waiting for him. Matteo froze from shock. He couldn't believe that one of the hottest producers in the business was standing right in front of him. His mouth stayed open for what seemed like hours. Chris walked over to him and held out his hand to shake. Matteo, still frozen, just stood there looking at him, with his mouth still open, until Brian nudged him. He finally came to himself and shook his hand and started stammering "You- you- you're Chris Thompson. I-I- It's such an honor to meet you".

"The honor and pleasure are all mine" Chris said as he slightly bowed his head while shaking his hand. "You were a HUGE surprise! I had no idea that Pastor Matthews had such talent in his family. Had I known, I would've been down here long before now! So, kid, how long have you been doing this and how much material do you have?"

Trying to collect his thoughts and get himself together, wanting to pinch himself to make sure he wasn't dreaming, Matteo managed to say "I have about 20 songs that are actually recorded, but I have way more that I've written. All I do is write. The songs just keep coming".

Chris reached in his jacket pocket and pulled out a card. "I think you have a lot of talent kid, and I'd like to hear more. Here's my business card. Call my office on Monday morning and we'll see what we can set up." Chris stretched his hand out to shake Matteo's hand, again, and Matteo slowly extended his back. Still in disbelief about what just happened, when Chris was far enough away, Matteo dropped to his knees, almost in tears. Although there was nothing concrete, yet, just the fact that a legend like Chris Thompson said he had a lot of talent and was interested in him, was more than he could've ever dreamed.

With so much excitement that he felt, it was like electricity was flowing all through his body, he ran with Brian in tow, to find his grandfather to tell him the good news. During all the chaos that was going on as the rally was being broken down and everybody was cleaning, he found his grandfather standing near the steps of the church talking to one of the Deacons of the church. All out of breath from running, Matteo yelled with excitement "Pop-Pop, Pop-Pop!! You'll never guess what just happened!! Chris Thompson said I had talent and he wants to meet with me and this could be the break I 've been looking for and who would ever think that I…."

"Wait, Wait! Slow down son and breathe! You're talking so fast I can't understand what you're saying. You know I'm an old man" Pop-Pop John said, jokingly. "Now, start from the beginning, and speak slowly".

"Chris Thompson, the legendary producer in hip hop, was here during my performance. He came up to me after everything was over and told me that he thinks I have a lot of talent and wants to hear my songs" he shouted excitedly, while shaking his grandfather's arm. "He wants to set up a meeting with me on Monday morning to listen to some more of my music to see if he wants to work with me! Isn't that AMAZING Pop-Pop??!!"

Pop-Pop John, of course, was not as thrilled about the whole idea as Matteo was. He didn't like, nor did he understand all that hip-hop stuff. All he knew (well what he thought he knew), was that hip hop was always associated with crime, gangs, and a lifestyle that he was trying desperately to keep Matteo from getting involved in. After all, according to Pop-Pop John, BOTH of Matteo's parents had fallen into that lifestyle and ended up drug addicts, and incarcerated. With all those thoughts in his mind, he felt it was his job as Matteo's legal guardian to be at any meeting that they decide to setup on Monday.

"Matteo, you know that I have to be at any meeting that they may want to have with you, right?" he asked, looking over the rim of his glasses, like he always did when he was serious about something. "I am your legal guardian and I am also your grandfather. It is my job to protect you, and in doing so, I must make sure that no one is going to take advantage of you or take any of your work without making sure you are fully compensated". He placed his hand on Matteo's shoulder, as he continued "I may not know hip hop, but I know a little bit about this music industry and the shadiness that can occur. I don't want you getting so caught up in the excitement of it all that you end up signing your life away for beans".

Matteo wasn't trying to hear any of what his grandfather was saying and just kept staring at the ground so that his grandfather couldn't see his eyes rolling. Pop-Pop John just kept going "Besides, I must make sure this guy's legit. So, this phone call that happens on Monday, better be in my presence and on speaker phone. I need to hear every detail from beginning to end"

"But Pop-Pop, Matteo pleaded, "He said that he knows you well. He said he used to go to Vacation Bible School here when he was growing up."

Pop-Pop John just stopped and glanced at him for a second before continuing to briskly walk through the parking lot to the side door where his office was. Before opening the door, he stopped, turned around towards Matteo who was following behind him, and continued.

"Do you know how many people have gone through this church throughout these years? A lot can change from the time that you're a kid to becoming an adult. People get jaded, they get mixed up in stuff that you wouldn't think they would and before you know it, you don't even know who they are anymore".

Matteo could tell that this was no longer about Chris, but about his father, John, Jr. "I don't want that to happen to you. So, we'll see about setting up this meeting, but please know that if there is one, I will be going with you or there will be no meeting, at all" he curtly stated as he opened and shut his office doors firmly behind him.

Feeling like all the wind had been let out of his sail, Matteo walked away completely different than he walked over. Brian tried to lift his spirits by saying, while patting him on the back "Matteo, he's your grandfather and you're not eighteen yet. I don't think it's a bad idea that he goes with you. You, yourself know how this industry can be". Brian always being the voice of reason, went on to say "It's better to have backup and support. That way you know you won't get played".

Walking slowly over to Brian's car with his head still down, Matteo responded "Yeah, but we also know how Pop-Pop feels about hip hop and the music industry, period. He thinks it's all an abomination. He'll find something wrong with everything they say or do. He'd better not ruin this for me". Matteo opened the passenger door and slumped down into the seat, as Brian got in on the driver's side. The drive home was silent.

It seemed like it took forever for Monday to come. Sunday service was like watching paint dry. It just seemed to drag on and on and on. Pop-Pop John didn't say one word about any of it all day Sunday. Matteo just knew that his grandfather was going to ruin this opportunity for him. He was hoping he would just forget about the phone call, but that was not the case at all.

At 9:57 am, Monday morning, in walked his grandfather. "Make sure you put that call on the speaker phone. I want to hear everything that's being said so there won't be any misunderstandings" he said as he sat down on Matteo's bed. Matteo turned his back to pick up the phone, while rolling his eyes. As he started dialing, he was so nervous that his hands were shaking. *What if he forgets who I am or changed his mind?* Matteo thought.

"Thank you for calling Rough Records Entertainment. This is Sheila speaking. How may I direct your call?" spoken by a highly professional sounding receptionist with a bit of a West Indies accent.

"Y-Yes." Matteo stammered, "My name is Matteo Matthews. I have a 10 o'clock conference call with Chris Thompson."

"Hold please" Sheila said with her Caribbean flavor, "Let me see if he is available". As Matteo waited, instead of elevator music playing as when most businesses put you on hold, all you heard were clips of Rough Records up and coming new artists. *OH MY GOD!! Yooo, these joints are lit!"* Matteo thought to himself. *Am I going to be able to hang with THEM?* He would soon find out. He knew if he was given the opportunity, he had to bring it.

"Matteo! My man! Right on time, just like I was hoping you would be". Chris reached over and shook Matteo's hand before sitting down. "One thing I can't stand is for somebody to waste my time and squander opportunity by being late 'cause then you messin with my money, and that's a sure-fire way to never get signed to my label. Now, let's get down to business."

Chris talked real fast as if his words were running away from him or something. Mateo had a hard time keeping up with him, but before they got into any business, Matteo, reluctantly, let him know that he was on speaker phone because his grandfather wanted to be in on the conversation to make sure everything was on the up and up. He was worried that Chris would think he was soft and a little kid and wouldn't take him seriously, but it was quite the contrary. He appreciated the fact that his grandfather was looking out for him. Chris was a father and said he would've done the same thing had his son or daughter wanted to get in the business.

"This game can be cutthroat. There are a lot of scam artists out here and a lot of people doing shady business deals, so your grandfather is right to be concerned, but everything's good here, Sir", he said, in an attempt to reassure him. "I have nothing but the utmost respect for you and for our artists. We tell all our potential artists upfront to make sure they have legal representation to look over their contracts because at the end of the day, we want our artists to know exactly what they're getting and what to expect so that we won't have to deal with frivolous lawsuits and people trying to hustle us out of money" Chris said with a slight chuckle. "We're all about making money, not losing here".

Once Pop-Pop John seemed satisfied with all that Chris was saying, Chris told Matteo that he wanted him to get about six or seven of his best songs together. He was going to have his secretary, Sheila, call him within the next couple of days to set up some studio time, and they would see what he had and if he had something they could work with. If they were interested and felt that they had the right connection and vibed right, he could potentially walk away as a new Rough Records Entertainment artist; of course, once all the legal matters were worked out.

Matteo was ecstatic when he got off the phone. His heart was beating a mile a minute. *Was this all a dream*, he thought to himself? As soon as he got off the phone, he hit up his boy Brian on the phone.

"Aye Yoooooo!!! I just got off the phone with Chris Thompson!! He wants me to come to the studios with six or seven of my hottest tracks to see if we vibe right in the studio and if it's something they wanna work with!!". Matteo was as animated as he could be, just bubbling over with excitement. "He said I could potentially walk away as a new artist on the Rough Records label!!" At that point, Matteo jumped up and down and literally screamed like a girl, "Do you KNOW HOW DOPE THAT WOULD BE???", he screamed. "When can I come over? We gotta get started. You know my joints gotta be RIGHT!!!".

"You can come over NOW, Bruh!" said Brian just as excited as Matteo was. "Nobody's home but me. Let's go!".

"Yo, I'm on THE way!". Matteo jumped in his car, he didn't even want to hear, nor did he care about what his grandfather had to say. He didn't want him to kill his vibe, right now. Brian's house was only a ten-minute drive, but it felt like it took an hour getting there to Matteo. He barely took the car out of gear and turned it off before he jumped out of it running in the house. They worked tirelessly, day and night, until it was time to go to the studios.

Thursday came, and it was time for him to go to the studios. Of course, his grandfather was not going to let him go alone. He just wished for one second, he would treat him like an adult. He was almost eighteen for God's sake. He was pretty much a man. When they pulled up to the studios, it wasn't what Matteo expected at all. The neighborhood was a bit grimy, it was a brick building that looked like it was antiquated. There were a few sketchy characters hanging around outside. He was almost glad that he didn't come by himself. It all looked a little "suspect".

As he was walking down the hallways, he was looking in the different rooms and seeing guys that looked like they were straight off the street; like they were still trappin. Some of them even looked like they were "packing" and probably were. Were they going to think he was soft; a church boy coming down there with his grandfather that's a pastor at that? He had to shake all of that off, because he had work to do. This was his only shot and he wasn't about to blow it.

Chris and two other guys were waiting for him in one of the rooms. There was a sound board set up on one side of the room where they were, headphones and a microphone on the other side of the plexiglass. As Chris introduced the other two guys, Jim Johns, and Dre Foster, his business partners, and producers, they wasted no time getting straight to work.

After four hours, they had heard all they needed to hear, and gave him an unofficial welcome to Rough Records. They were convinced that he had what they were looking for and informed him that once they had the paperwork drawn up, and he had his lawyers check it out, they were ready to put him to work. They wanted to start him with a single, and if that went well, they would put out an EP. The day he signed that contract was the day he lost all the innocence that he had.

Lying there on that gurney, he started flashing back to all the days his grandmother took him to church, the sermons his grandfather preached, the days in school when he had his little friends, and everything was just fun and carefree. He wanted to go back to those days so bad, but how could he go back to that now? He had done too much damage and burned too many bridges. Once he started getting the fame, the women came, the ego came, and he forgot about everybody that was there when he had nothing. He and Brian hadn't talked for about a year and a half. He had disrespected his grandparents when they saw him going down the wrong path. They had seen it before and had gone through the same thing with Matteo's father.

Matteo couldn't believe his last words to his grandfather was "I hate you! You never wanted me to be anything but be like YOU!". He broke his grandparents' hearts. He started drinking and smoking weed to numb the pain of being lonely; not knowing who he could trust or who was there just for his fame and money. When the girls, the weed, and the alcohol didn't work, he was introduced to the next level of "high"; cocaine and heroin while he was touring.

Matteo, well Kilo, now, would look in the mirror and not even know who he was anymore. He was no longer Matteo. His life was slipping away. His grandparents could see it every time they saw him on TV, but they would have to turn because it would be too painful for them to watch. He was nineteen, now. There was nothing that they could do. He had his own home and made his own money. He was a grown man; at least that's how Matteo saw it.

As he closed his eyes, Matteo started flatlining again. This time he saw the brightest light he had ever seen. He saw an angel that told him it wasn't time for him to go yet and that he still had work to do, but if he didn't turn his life around, he would be back to get him, soon. Suddenly, it became pitch black and he saw a fire with hands reaching out and people crying out "You don't want to come here! You don't want to come here!". Right at that moment it was like a jolt of lightening had hit his body. There was a heartbeat.

As Matteo lay their unconscious for the next few days, he heard his grandparents talking to him and praying for him. He heard the doctors talking to them. He couldn't respond, but he could hear everything. There was one moment when the room was silent. His grandparents must've gone home to get some rest or something. It was just silent.

Matteo suddenly heard the door open and felt a presence sitting beside his bed. They didn't say anything, but Matteo knew they were there. He felt them place something in his hand. When their hand touched his, Matteo opened his eyes for the first time.

It was a little blurry and at first, he had a hard time focusing his eyes, but just as he looked over, he saw the silhouette of a man walking out of the door. When his eyes finally focused enough, he read what appeared to be a business card of some kind. There was only an address, date, and time on it. Just then, the door opened, and a nurse walked in. Surprised to see him awake, she went to go get the doctor, which gave Matteo time to slip the card in his wallet. He was intrigued and wanted to know who it was and what they wanted.

7 THE FURIOUS FATHER

Standing over his son in the middle of Pinnacle Street, watching the blood ooze from his head, Hakeem just dropped to his knees, sobbing inconsolably. He picked his son up and just held him in his arms like a baby, while onlookers were watching in disbelief, anger, and grieving with the single father. The people that were sworn to protect and serve had now become the enemy to a whole community. They were all confused. Some were there and saw what happened, as they stood by whispering and watching to see what would happen next.

The officers on the scene would not go near the grieving father or his son for fear of what Hakeem would do and what the crowd of people would do. They knew Hakeem's history and did not know what state of mind he was in and how he would respond to them in this moment. It was an extremely sensitive situation. The atmosphere was so charged with emotions that it was almost impossible to breathe.

Hakeem was in a state of shock. He sat there for almost two hours, holding his son thinking of the last things that he had said to his son. It wasn't the proper protocol for the Investigators to allow anyone to tamper with any evidence and especially not the victim. None of the officers, however, wanted to be the one to tell Hakeem that he had to leave his son in their care; especially not after what had just occurred.

Every day Hakeem would tell his son to be careful out there because every little thing he did was being watched and scrutinized; not because he was under surveillance or had been in any trouble, but simply because he was a young black man and because he was Hakeem's son. Unfortunately, it started to appear that the times had reversed back to pre-Civil Rights Movement days, on so many levels. Black men were again, blatantly being targeted and killed. It had never really stopped, it just hadn't been as intensified as it was now, since then.

While it was true that the neighborhood that Hakeem and his son had lived in was a rough neighborhood, most of the guys that were doing all the illegal stuff around there, knew and respected Hakeem and had always watched out for his son, J'son. Hakeem had been raised in the streets. Hakeem's father spent most of Hakeem's life locked up, so he never had a relationship with his father and as he grew up, he became, unknowingly, more and more like his father.

Hakeem was infamous in the streets, and had a reputation for being extremely dangerous, but once J'son came into the picture, he realized he had to make some changes in his life. He didn't want J'son growing up without a father the way he did.

J'son's mother, Kisha, became an exotic dancer shortly after high school, which is where Hakeem met her. During that time, Hakeem was becoming known as a heavy hitter. They lived a fast and wild life. Kisha quickly became known as Hakeem's number one girl. While there were several other girls that he had sex with, Kisha was the one he claimed as "his girl". She loved being "his girl" too, because he lavished her with all kinds of expensive gifts.

Kisha loved attention, which is why she loved exotic dancing. She loved the fact that all eyes were on her and she did like having her own money. Hakeem tried many times to get her to stop, but when she refused, he would just make sure he controlled when she danced and for whom. When Kisha became pregnant with J'son, she did not want to stop dancing and shortly after she had him, she got right back up there as soon as she could.

A few months before J'son's first birthday, Kisha met an NFL football player, named Rick Montana. He had recently bought the club that she worked for, but when he started taking a liking to her, he told her he wanted her to stop stripping and be his girl and leave Hakeem and his "gangsta" lifestyle alone before she ends up dead or in prison, like Hakeem was sure to end up.

Rick filled her head with all sorts of piped dreams of how he could give her the world and all she saw were dollar signs. Rick had another house in Miami that he would spend most of his time in, and only flew in town to Maryland when he needed to take care of some business. He had a private jet, and he had way more clout and prestige than Hakeem ever could. He promised Kisha that he would buy her a strip club of her own, down in Miami. It did not take long before she left Hakeem and left J'son, too.

One day, Hakeem came home, the home that he and Kisha shared, to find J'son strapped in his car seat, with a bottle in his hand and a note attached to him that read:

Dear Hakeem, I never wanted to be a mother and give up on my dreams. At first, being with you made me feel like you were the one for me and would be the one to support and help to build my dreams. Being with you with the possibility of you going to jail and leaving me alone with a kid to take care of, is not going to work for me. I met someone that has promised to help me to become the person that I've always known I could be and can afford to give J'son and me the life that you can't. I will come back for J'son when I get myself set up.

Neither Hakeem or J'son heard from Kisha again. While it was an adjustment, at first, Hakeem knew, at that moment, that he had to give up the street life. He didn't want J'son angry and bitter like he and his father were. He wanted him to be happy and at peace. He wanted to end that generational curse.

Working a regular job was extremely difficult for Hakeem, at first. He was used to making fast money, but he knew he had to do whatever he had to do to be an example for his son. He never wanted his son to feel for one second that he wasn't loved or wanted because of what his mother did. Hakeem was well on his way to accomplishing all the he had hoped to with J'son.

J'son was a great kid. He was an honor roll student, the star baseball player at his high school, and the President of the Student Government. J'son also believed in wanting to better his community and spearheaded several projects to rebuild the area within his community that had been deteriorating. His girlfriend, Joy, was a sweetheart and one of the top students in their class, just like J'son.

Everyone in the community saw J'son going places and was rooting for him to make a name for himself. Growing up, Hakeem had J'son in every camp or after school program he could, just to keep him busy and off the streets. He knew, all too well, how enticing the fast life could be.

When J'son was younger, he never realized how much they were struggling financially, but as he got older, he understood how difficult things were and how hard his father was working for him. He didn't want to disappoint him, so he worked hard to be the best at everything he did, and he was. He was on his way to a full scholarship with Morehouse College; not on a baseball scholarship, but an academic scholarship. Now, all the hard work Hakeem had done to make sure his son had a better life than he did, was gone; all his hopes, dreams, aspirations were gone, and he felt nothing but pure rage inside. He wanted to make whoever did this to his son, feel the same pain he felt.

Finally laying his son down so that the coroner could come and take his body and the CSI team could complete their investigation, Hakeem, just walked away, slowly. He had the look of hatred on his face when any uniform came in his direction. He didn't want anyone talking to him; especially not the cops. They were the reason his son was lying in the streets, with a bullet in his head; dead. He didn't want to hear anything they had to say.

Hakeem knew his son. He was respectful and was always taught to respect the police officers that patrolled their neighborhood daily. Those same officers knew him and knew that J'son was a good kid, and even commended Hakeem for how he turned his life around and raised J'son. So how did this happen? He knew that there was nothing that his son could've done that would've warranted him to be shot in his head and killed by anyone, let alone a police officer in their own neighborhood. As J'son's body laid cold in the middle of the street, Hakeem wanted answers, and he was determined to get them, but not from the cops. Somebody was going to have to pay.

The next day, Hakeem was sitting in the police station; not because he wanted to, but because he had to. He needed answers. He knew they would have no answers for him and he didn't want to hear anymore lies from them about why his son is dead. The longer he sat there, the more furious he grew by the minute. He couldn't fathom how thousands of white boys had been disarmed and unharmed for whatever crimes they had committed, no matter how heinous they were, but for some reason, he, like all the other parents and family members of black teenage boys, girls, and men that were killed unjustly, find themselves left with no answers and no justice.

"Mr. Turner, we told you already, Sir, there isn't much you can do here. We are investigating what happened. We're doing everything we can to make sure we find out what happened last night, but right now, we don't have any answers to give you". The Police Chief, Captain Smith, continued from afar off, in an agitated voice. "Please go home, Sir. We will let you know the minute we have any new information for you". He turned his back on Hakeem and swiftly began to walk away.

Hakeem was persistent, following right on his heels. Like a tea kettle that steamed over, Hakeem's anger just took over "I'm not leaving until somebody tells me why my son is lying on a cold slab with a hole in his head by one of your officers!!" he yelled, lunging after Captain Smith.

As two of the other officers grabbed him to hold him back, one officer jumped in front of Captain Smith as he said in a frustrated manner, "Sir, please go home. I would hate to have you arrested for assaulting a police officer". At that moment, Hakeem realized that being there wouldn't solve anything. They wouldn't tell him anything even if they knew something. Those officers would get off for killing his son, just like all the others had. Hakeem thought to himself *I'll find a way to get the justice I deserve, but I'm not going to wait for the justice system to get it.*

On the other side of town, a young man sat on the edge of his bed with his head in his hands, crying and rocking back and forth. He had never had to draw his gun on anyone, let alone pull the trigger. Now, there's a kid lying in the morgue with a bullet in his head; his bullet. *How could I take the life of an innocent kid*, he asked himself? *What if it was one of my kids*, he thought, as he stretched out across the bed sobbing.

Officer Frank Best had just recently graduated from the police academy six months prior and was new to the area. Fresh out of the academy and into the fire, as the turmoil between cops and the black communities was on an all-time high and he was now right in the thick of it. If he could change what happened in that moment, he would.

The truth is, Frank was scared. There was so much going on in that neighborhood, at that time. There was a riot that had broken out over a convenient store owner racially profiling his customers. Some of the people in the neighborhood were fed up and decided to boycott and were picketing the store. The store owner came outside shouting racial slurs and epithets which caused some of the people in the crowd to get red with fury. That anger turned into violence as someone threw a trash can through the window and then charged the store, beating the store owner. Gunshots rang out and everyone started running frantically.

By the time the cops arrived, everyone had dispersed, and the shooters were nowhere to be found.

The cops surveyed the neighborhood looking for the person that fit the description that the store owner gave: black teen with gray hooded sweatshirt and sweatpants, about 5'8" tall, with dark skin. As the cops drove around, they saw a kid that they thought fit the description and yelled for the boy to stop. As the boy kept walking, with his hands in his pockets, the cops drew their weapons. Finally noticing that he was being followed, he turned around and noticed that there were cops behind him with their guns drawn. When the boy went to pull his hands out of his pocket to put them up, Officer Best shot him, instantly; right in the middle of the forehead.

It wasn't until the kid stopped moving that Officer Best realized he had earphones on and was listening to music and that was the reason that he couldn't hear them. They searched his pockets and saw that he had no weapons. Officer Best was devastated, and there were witnesses that caught the whole incident on video. Officer Best's partner, Officer Wilkins, confiscated their cameras, but it was already online. They called the incident in and when back up came, they sent Officer Best back to the station, feeling that it was too dangerous for him to be there and wanting to prep him for what was to come. Shortly after, Hakeem arrived on the scene.

With nothing but rage driving him, Hakeem started canvassing the neighborhood to find out what his neighbors knew. He wanted the details from the people that he trusted the most; his street family. Those are the ones that have had his and J'son's back from day one. Those were the ones that have looked after him, while

Hakeem worked tirelessly to keep a roof over their heads and to make sure J'son had everything he needed to succeed. They were the ones that would help him get to the bottom of this; not those pigs that lie and do anything to protect their own.

Hakeem saw several people sitting on their porches, that just nodded as he walked by. He knew what that nod meant; "we got you". The first house he walked up to, was the lady they call "neighborhood watch". Her name was Ms. Carpenter. There was no official neighborhood watch in their community, but if anything went down around there, she always knew about it. She never missed anything.

Before he could even get to her front door, she met him at the doorway. Standing there with rollers still in her hair, in her ratty peach terry-clothed robe, thick lensed glasses (that you could see Mars through), and arms outstretched. "Come on in, sugah" as she grabbed him and squeezed him like a lemon. "Ms. Carpenter's been praying for you all night. Ms. Carpenter was hoping she'd get a chance to see you today. How are you holdin up, baby"? She always talked about herself in third-person for some reason. No one ever understood why, but after she had done it for so long, no one ever questioned it anymore.

"Good morning, Ms. Carpenter. I'm trying to hang in there. Still in shock, just trying to wrap my head around everything. That's why I'm here. I was wondering if you saw anything that happened last night? The police won't tell me anything and I need to know what happened to my son" he asked, fighting back the tears. He was trying to hold it together as best he could. The last thing he wanted to do was break down in her house. The whole neighborhood would know it and there would have been a few embellishments added to it.

As Ms. Carpenter began to talk, she led him to the couch and sat him down. "Well, Ms. Carpenter was outside sitting on the porch, like she always does. Ms. Carpenter saw your boy walking down the street with his headphones on" she said motioning in the direction that he was walking from. "guess he had just got back from practice or something, when these cops pulled up behind him, turned off the lights, and parked the car. They got out of the car, but I don't think J'son saw or heard them because, like Ms. Carpenter said, he had his headphones on and you know how loud these children have their music in their ears. It's a wonder they can hear anything at all".

Hakeem wasn't interested in all of that. He just wanted to get to the part about how his son got shot. Trying to rush her along, he interjected "Ms. Carpenter, what happened after that? How did my son get shot? Did he resist them? Did he lunge towards them or put up any kind of fight or confrontation with them in any way that would make them need to shoot him?"

Ms. Carpenter wrinkled up her face as if she was trying to think real hard. "No. The cops were yelling at him to turn around and get down on the ground with his hands up. I don't think he even heard them. He saw someone pointing at him to turn around, but as he reached down to turn his music down and turn around to look at what they were pointing at, they shot him. It all happened so fast. The one cop yelled at the other cop and asked him why he shot him, and the cop that shot him said that he thought he had a gun".

Hakeem winced at the thought of his son getting shot and it was almost like he blacked out. Ms. Carpenter was still talking, but he couldn't hear anything past his own blind fury at that point. Once he snapped out of it, he asked Ms. Carpenter if she remembered which cop had shot him. She thought she had only seen him once before and could describe him in great details, young, kind of tall and lanky, but didn't know his name.

Hakeem stood up, and gave Ms. Carpenter a hug, thanking her for the information. After her description, he knew just who she was talking about. As Hakeem started out the door, she yelled out that she would send him some food over by her grandson because she knew he would need to eat. That's what that neighborhood did; took care of each other.

It was just like Hakeem had thought. He knew his son. He knew J'son would never do anything to disrespect law enforcement or do anything to break the law. He had the same talk with J'son that most black parents, unfortunately, have had to have with their children; especially their sons: *Stay out of trouble. If a cop stops you, say yes Sir, or Ma'am, No Sir or Ma'am. Do whatever they ask you to do, whether you think it's the right thing to do or not. Never make any sudden movements, if they ask for your ID, let them know where it is and where you must go to reach for it because whatever you do, you cannot put your hands in your pockets or anywhere out of clear view without informing them, first. Don't walk away from them and don't walk towards them. Don't resist them in any way.*

He knew his son couldn't have heard the cops because he had always obeyed his father and done what he had to do to make it home safely. This wasn't J'son's first time being harassed by the cops. Hakeem knew what kind of neighborhood he was in and how the people that didn't live there, viewed their black boys. He instilled in J'son from birth to do whatever he had to, to make sure he got home safely. Now all those talks seemed to have been in vain. His boy was dead and by the hands of those that "swore" to protect and serve. J'son was safer with the gangs in the streets.

When Hakeem got back in his house, he got a call from a representative of the NAACP. They wanted to provide legal services and any type of support they felt he may need. They had been fighting these battles for decades and weren't afraid to fight against the judicial system or the legal systems to get the results that he and other parents of slain sons, daughters, mothers, and fathers deserved. The people began to rally around Hakeem and his lawyers as they addressed the issues and the plans that they were seeking to hold the officers accountable for their actions.

Unfortunately, black communities nationwide, had seen these types of incidents happening too many times before and knew the steps that would be taken by the police department and the judicial system: 1. The officers would be placed on PAID administrative leave (i.e. a paid vacation), 2. Information on the victim's criminal past would be leaked to the press, in which they would try to demonize the victim or the victims' family (as if to say they somehow deserved to die the way they did), 3. They would charge the officers (mainly to quiet down the community or city because there have been protests), 4. Evidence will somehow fail to appear in court or be considered "inadmissible" to the court, 5. No one in the community will get questioned and if they do, they won't be considered viable witnesses, and finally, 6. The cops will be exonerated of all charges and the parents and families will be left with no answers and no justice.

Hakeem did what his lawyers suggested. He made statements for the press that were delivered by his representatives, however, Hakeem had his own agenda. He had no trust or confidence in the judicial system or in the police department. After nine months of doing what he was told to do, watching everything unfold just the way that he knew it would, the cop that shot his son got exonerated. They claimed that when they yelled at J'son to put his hands up and turn around, that he was being defiant. He wasn't doing what they asked him to do and then as he was turning around, they thought he was reaching for a gun and he felt he had to protect himself. The other cop that was with him corroborated his story, although he questioned his actions at the scene. They didn't even want to hear what those within the neighborhood that had seen it happen, had to say.

Hakeem's lawyers said they would appeal the decision and take it to a higher court, but he wasn't interested in that. He wasn't interested in wasting anymore of his time with a judicial system that he didn't trust. He was going to go back to what he knew best; the streets. If he couldn't get justice one way, he knew another way he could get it and too many people that would be glad to help him.

"Yo" said the raspy voice on the other end of the phone. Hakeem had called his number one man from back in the day; Orlando, A.K.A. the Eraser. He was called the Eraser because by the time he was finished with someone, it was as though they had never existed or at least they'd wish they hadn't. He always told Hakeem that whenever he needed him, he'd be there no matter what.

"Get the boys together. I need a job done" was all Hakeem said before hanging up. They knew exactly where to meet and when. They already had a plan in place in case there was ever an emergency and Hakeem needed them. He had done everything he had to, to stay away from the street life and give J'son opportunities that he never had, but they had always been lying dormant inside of him. Now that J'son was gone, Hakeem felt that he had nothing to live for anymore. He was going to avenge his son's death, even if that meant meeting his own.

Lying there in the bed, looking up at the ceiling, all he could do was hear his son's laughter and see his face. It made him smile for a second, until he remembered the last time he held his son; limp, bloody, and lifeless. Then the rage returned. He went to the refrigerator and grabbed a cold beer; sat at the table and did something he hadn't done in years. He got his emergency stash of weed out, rolled a joint, and smoked it. He smoked and drank until he passed out.

Hakeem wanted to be numb. He didn't want to feel anything or even think. He sobered up long enough to make the arrangements for J'son's funeral, with the help of his sister Lulu and his mother Linda, the next day. They wanted to stay with him, and desperately tried to stay, knowing that he didn't need to be alone, but Hakeem made it clear that he didn't want anyone in the house with him; he needed time to get his thoughts together and figure out what to do next.

At J'son's funeral, the High-Street Baptist church was packed with wall-to-wall people; J'son's coaches, friends, teachers, people in the community, and family were all present. Even J'son's mother, Kisha, came, but she sat all the way in the back, where no one could see her; riddled with guilt for having left them. Her heart broke, but more for Hakeem. She knew how much he loved their son, and how much he had given up making sure that he had the best future possible. She knew that Hakeem was strong, but that this may be the one thing that broke him.

There were so many wonderful things that were being said about J'son, however, Hakeem didn't hear any of it. He couldn't stop staring at that coffin and realizing his son was in there; dead. *What did I do wrong?* he thought to himself. *Maybe I shouldn't have worked so many hours, maybe if I had been there more, this wouldn't have happened. Maybe my past is finally catching up to me.* He just couldn't fathom why God would allow his son, that he worked so hard to keep out of trouble, to die in such a tragic way, at such an early age, and by the ones that were supposed to protect him. All this time he was so worried about the streets killing J'son, and it seems he should've been even more worried about the cops.

The whole time that the pastor preached, the choir sang, people cried, and laughed telling funny stories about J'son, all Hakeem could think about was killing the man that did this to his son. He didn't want him to die; he wanted him to kill him on the inside. He wanted him to feel what he felt; what it was like to lose a child. He wanted him to know the pain and anguish that came from losing the one person that was the closest thing to his heart. He wanted him to try to pick up the pieces of his life and feel what it felt like to wake up every day knowing that his actions caused him to lose his everything in one moment, and that moment was quickly approaching.

On the eve of the "Day of Reckoning", the day that all the plans that he and the "Eraser" had put together was supposed to go down, J'son came to him in a dream. He simply saw his face and heard his voice saying "Dad, please don't do this. This isn't the way. I will never be at peace until you are, and this won't bring you peace. This won't bring me back. Don't throw your life away. Honor my memory by showing other boys in the neighborhood without fathers, how you fathered me. You were the greatest dad. Others need to feel the love that I felt; those who don't have fathers to love them back." Then, just like that, he was gone, and Hakeem woke up startled and sweating. He thought about those words and just wept incessantly.

Hakeem dragged himself to the bathroom, stumbling in the dark to splash his face with water to get himself together. As he was preparing to strap up and go meet with the guys, while he was getting dressed, all he kept hearing were the words that his son spoke. He tried desperately to drown out the voice of his son in his head, however, it just wouldn't go away, but it wasn't going to stop him. He had to avenge his son's death; even if it was the last thing he ever did.

As Hakeem met up with the guys, they were ready. The Eraser asked Hakeem "Are you sure you want to do this because there's no turning back from this?" More determined than ever, Hakeem looked at the Eraser and said with a dark tone to his voice "ain't no going back. I got nothing to lose, but that pig is about to feel everything I'm feeling right now. He's gonna know what it's like to have a child taken from him"

As they pulled up to Officer Best's home, all the lights were out. They had done their homework. They knew exactly which room Officer Best's son's was. They weren't going to harm the child, just kidnap him and keep his father terrified. They just wanted him to see how it felt to fear that his child would never be returning home again.

Hakeem pulled the screen off the window and jimmied the window open. He climbed through the window and just as he was about to pick Officer Best's son up, Officer Best walked in the room and for a moment, they locked eyes, staring intently at one another. Hakeem looked down at the sleeping child and back up at Officer Best with the most sinister smile. Officer Best quietly begged Hakeem not to take his son. He knew exactly who Hakeem was. Officer Best continued as he moved slowly toward them, trying not to make sudden moves, "Please. Just leave him alone and take me instead. I deserve it, he doesn't. He is innocent".

"Innocent? You mean just like my boy was?!" Hakeem was even more driven to continue with his plan, once he saw the fear in Officer Best's eyes. That was exactly what he wanted to see. Then, suddenly, out of nowhere Hakeem heard his son's voice again. Hakeem was frozen for what seemed like forever. The boy woke up and looked up Hakeem and screamed for his father. Hakeem began to come to himself. *What am I doing? I'm not this person anymore.* As he slowly put the boy back down on the bed, he fell to his knees.

Officer Best, not knowing what to do, just remained quiet and still as his son scurried over to him. He didn't want to say anything to anger Hakeem. Hakeem put his wrists out for Officer Best to arrest him, but Officer Best just told him to go home. "We can just pretend that this never even happened".

Officer Best was sincere, and Hakeem could see that in that moment, they were two fathers that deeply loved their sons and were more alike than he realized. He also saw the regret and sheer pain in Officer's Best's eyes for killing J'son. The young father didn't want to bring any more pain to Hakeem than he already had.

As Hakeem climbed out the window and went back to the car, the Eraser was asking "where's the boy?" as he tried to stop Hakeem. "What happened?". Hakeem just got back in the car and told the Eraser to just drive. He rode back home in total silence. He couldn't wrap his mind around what just happened. It was like he had an outer body experience. It wasn't him. As much as he thought he was, he just wasn't that person anymore.

When Hakeem got home, he just knelt beside his bed to do something he hadn't done in a very long time; probably since he was a child. He began to pray. As he started pleading to God to help him deal with all the pain, he noticed this bright red card just randomly lying beside his bed. He picked it up and read it.......

8 THE TORTURED TRANSGENDER

Overlooking the Inner Harbor in downtown Baltimore, was one of the most beautiful and unique Spanish style mansions on the east coast; ten luxurious bedrooms, and nine spa-like bathrooms. The electronic, iron gates opened, and the driveway led to the elaborate hand-carved, wooden doors that seemed to reach to the heavens. Behind those doors lived the De Lucca family. The De Lucca family was one of the wealthiest families on the East Coast, owning one of the largest construction companies; De Lucca Construction, Inc.

Anthony De Lucca, Sr. was a migrant from Sicily. He started the company from nothing, but by the time Anthony De Lucca, Jr., was ready to take over the company, business was booming. Under the leadership of Anthony De Lucca, Jr., the company had more than quadrupled its revenue and had branched out to six different states on the East coast. Anthony, Jr. was hoping that his son, Anthony De Lucca, III, would be ready to take the company even further than he did; however, Anthony (Tony, as he liked to be called), had other plans in mind.

It was Tony's last summer before he headed off to college. He couldn't wait. He loved his family, but at times, his family could be extremely overbearing. They were the typical Italian family. Tony was the only boy out of the four children. He was the youngest, and he was the one that had the most pressure; not only because they were counting on him to run the family business when he finished college, but it was because they expected him to one day do something that he would never do; marry a woman and have children of his own to carry on the family name and legacy. Tony wanted children someday, but he was not sure he would ever want them with another woman. The thing was, they had no idea that Tony desired to be Toni; a woman.

All of Tony's life, he had watched his sisters and his mother do their hair, put on makeup, talk about girl things, and he'd always felt like he could identify more with them than with his father, uncles, and male cousins. They always talked about sports, women, and the business. Tony never wanted to play any sports, and he wasn't any good at the ones his father forced him to play. He was harassed by his uncles and cousins; they called him a sissy and said that he threw like a girl.

Two of Tony's male cousins used to beat him up all the time because their fathers all thought that would toughen him up. He HATED family gatherings on Sundays because it always meant torture for him. He felt that, finally, once he was in college, he would be away from his family and would be able to be himself. The only person in the family that knew of his desire to transition into a woman was his oldest sister, Bella.

Bella had always been Tony's sounding board. He always talked to Bella about everything. She had always been very nurturing and was the least judgmental out of his family; besides, she was the one that found him trying on her clothes and makeup one day. He felt he had no choice but to come clean.

Bella was great when he told her. She said she had already had a feeling that something was going on, but that she was glad that he felt he could trust her with something so intimate. It meant a lot to them both that he could lean on her. The only other person that Tony felt he could confide in was his childhood friend, Cyprus Cappriziano.

Cyprus and Tony were like two peas in a pod since they were four years old. They met through their parents that had become close friends through a business venture. Cyprus was this plump, green-eyed, raven haired girl that had a crooked smile. Her parents said that she wasn't the cutest, so they had her dressed up in these frilly clothes that made her look like a doll baby to compensate for what she lacked in looks.

By the time Tony and Cyprus got to middle school, they were stuck together like glue. They were both targets of bullying because Tony acted too girly and Cyprus was chunky with braces and acne. The two of them never saw the other's flaws. All they saw was someone that stuck up for them and wanted to be their friend no matter what. All they had was each other. It also helped having Cyprus around because his parents just assumed that she was his "little girlfriend" because they did everything together.

During their sophomore year, Cyprus and Tony were hanging out at Cyprus's house after school, laying on her bed, looking up at the ceiling, listening to music as they always did, when suddenly, Cyprus turned her face towards Tony and tried to kiss him. It startled him, at first, because he had never thought about kissing anyone in that way before and he certainly never thought about kissing Cyprus. As he quickly pulled away from her, she started to cry. "Cy, why are you crying? It just caught me off guard" Tony uttered.

"You think I'm ugly, too, don't you?" she cried. "Just like everybody else thinks I'm fat and ugly" she said as she began to sob.

Tony gently stroked her hair and said "It's not that at all, Cy. I think you are one of the most beautiful and amazing people I know" he reassured her.

"Then why won't you kiss me?" she asked.

"It's not what you think." He said as he took a long deep breath. "Cy, there's something I have to tell you". As he sat up in Indian style on the bed and looked down at his shoes, fumbling with the shoestrings, he said "I don't know how you're going to react." He took in another deep breath. Cyprus impatiently yelled "just spit it out!" and he did just that.

With his eyes closed, Tony attempted to express his feelings in a way that he would have the least amount of backlash. "Cy, I want to be a girl, and I've always wanted to be a girl and I think, but I'm not quite sure, that I like boys or maybe that I think I should like them because I feel like a girl. I don't know." he said in one long sentence.

Relieved that he finally told her, but anxious about what she was going to say and how she was going to react, he slowly opened his eyes to see what kind of reaction she had on her face. He was completely shocked to see what he saw. There she was, her tears had turned into an angry scowl. He didn't know what to think. All he knew was at that moment, he wished he could swallow those words back into his mouth and pretend he'd never said them because the look on her face said that she wanted to murder him!

"I don't believe you!" she screamed. "I can't believe you would make up a lie like that just to avoid telling me how you really feel; that I'm fat and ugly!". She REALLY broke down into inconsolable tears, then.

Tony threw his hands up in protest "Wait! No! Why would I lie and say something like THAT just so that I wouldn't hurt your feelings? I'm telling you the truth!" he yelled at the top of his lungs. Cyprus ran to the door, tears streaming down her face and flung the door open and motioned him to leave.

As Tony reluctantly walked to the door he looked her in the face and asked her "You've never had a feeling that something was going on?" As he put his head down, he said one last thing to her "I thought you knew me better than anybody" and walked out the door. He literally felt like he just lost his best and ONLY friend he had ever had.

Days had gone by and Tony hadn't heard a word from Cyprus. By now, he thought, for sure she would've called, but she didn't. He was so afraid that she would tell everyone his secret. He would see her at school, and she would just ignore him and keep walking by him as if he didn't even exist. He didn't know what to do. He felt so lost and alone.

This went on for two weeks, until his phone rang, and it was Cyprus on the other end. "Listen Tony, I don't like the way that we left things. Can you come over, so we can talk?". A little apprehensive about what he was walking into, but desperately hoping to get his friend back, he hesitated before agreeing.

As Tony arrived at her house, the first thing Cyprus did was hugged him and said, "I'm sorry". That somewhat eased his mind, but he was still a bit cautious. She went on to say, sitting down on her bed beside him "I was hurt, at first. I just KNEW you felt the same way that I did".

Cyprus gently placed her hand in Tony's hand and said in a soft voice, "I knew I had never heard you talk about any other girls before. I just thought, maybe, you just adored me. I mean, I AM great!" she said, with a nervous sort of laughter. "Besides, you are one of the kindest people I know. I wouldn't be a friend if I only liked you for what I thought you should be and not who you wanted to be". She reached both of her arms out to suggest a hug.

As she pulled him in close, she whispered in his ear "I just want you to be happy with being you". *This is the girl*, Tony thought to himself, *that I know and love*. "Have you told anyone else?" She asked him.

"Just Bella. She's known for a while and has always been a support to me. I just don't know what to do. My parents could NEVER know this. It would KILL them". He sat there for a moment in silence, staring off into space before continuing. "I should just keep it our secret, for now. In the meantime, they think that you're my girlfriend, so my dad and uncles don't harass me about girls".

"Well, I don't mind pretending to be your girlfriend", Cyprus says. "Who else is gonna want me now, anyway?" she said pretending to joke, but feeling that way deep down. Her self-esteem was already low but realizing that the only boy that she thought had feelings for her caused it to plummet even more.

During the following summer, however, between Tony and Cyprus's junior and senior year, Tony started to see Cyprus changing. She started eating healthier and was obsessed with working out. She wanted to lose weight. She was determined to go to school in her senior year and have the best year ever. Her braces came off, and the ugly duckling had started to become a beautiful swan. She no longer wanted to hang around Tony as much. She confided in him that she wanted a real boyfriend; someone that liked her and wanted to be with her in the same way.

Cyprus assured Tony that they would remain close friends, and they did for a little while. They still spent a lot of time together, just not as much. It didn't take long, unfortunately, before she had a boyfriend and she felt that she had to start putting a little distance between them to prove that they weren't in a romantic relationship. She didn't want her new boyfriend to be suspicious of them hanging out all the time or having to admit that he wasn't even into girls like that.

Quickly into their senior year, Cyprus was no longer in a cocoon, but she had spread her wings and became the social butterfly. She joined the dance team and talked Tony into it as well. Although his father, his uncles, and some of the guys at school made fun of him for dancing, he played the macho role and said he did it, so he could be around all those girls and have his pick of women. He wasn't sure if they believed him or not, but they left him alone, and he was happy about that because he loved to dance; and was good at it!

Tony's senior year seemed to fly by, and he couldn't wait to go away to college. All he could think of was going to Miami; somewhere where no one knew him, having a fresh start, and being his true self. No more hiding; at least while he was at school.

When the fall finally arrived, all the family went with Tony to make sure he was all settled in at college. His father pulled him aside, placed his hand on his shoulder while handing Tony a stash of condoms, and said "Son, be responsible. You know you have a legacy to protect. No diseases, no illegitimate children. We're the De Luccas. We have a reputation to uphold." He then leaned down, because Anthony De Lucca was a giant of a man, grabbed his son's face with both hands, and kissed him on the cheek.

It killed Tony that his parents thought they knew him but had no clue of who he was. They all gave him one last hug, his mother in tears at the thought of letting her baby go and climbed into the truck. At that moment, when he could no longer see that SUV, he let out the biggest "YES!!!" he could muster up, jumping up clicking his heels. He was FINALLY free; at least while he was there.

The first thing that Tony did, was set his room up. When he walked in, the cement floors and plain white walls looked like a prison especially compared to the palace that he came from. Fortunately, Tony had requested a single room, so he didn't have to worry about having any roommates and could decorate his room exactly the way he wanted to. He never could've decorated his room the way he had always wanted to at home, because he had to continue with the façade for his family.

Tony's room at home was extremely masculine with lots of dark wood, blues, and grays, which to him, just seemed plain old boring. He loved color, and bright colors at that; reds, oranges, turquoise, and deep purple. Those colors were bold, beautiful, vibrant, and made him feel alive! So, the moment he was all checked into his room, he called a car service, and went to the nearest department store he could find.

Tony was somewhat shy. He had a difficult time making friends because he didn't know who he could trust and who he could be himself with. He hated being fake and he hated being labeled as gay at school. He had never even had a relationship with anyone, let alone a sexual relationship with anyone to know what he felt his sexual orientation was. He was too busy struggling with his gender identification.

It frustrated Tony that so many people just felt that identifying as the opposite sex meant that you were automatically homosexual. *Sexuality has nothing to do with what gender a person identifies as* he would always think to himself whenever he would overhear conversations from others speaking about transgender individuals. Tony just felt like a female trapped inside the body of a male. He just wanted his outside to match his inside.

Once the semester started, Tony met Daisy; a girl that was in his chemistry class. Daisy ended up being his lab partner and they seemed to hit it off well. She was kind, and nurturing; a lot like his sister, Bella. Daisy was beautiful. She was what his father (who can be extremely tactless, at times) would've called, a half breed (half Caucasian, half African American).

Daisy had the roundest light brown eyes, and her skin looked like French vanilla cappuccino, the perfect blend, with the cutest freckles on her face. Her hair was like honey blonde and light brown perfectly swirled ringlets that were just strewn all over her head; just as wild and carefree as she was. They laughed a lot in class; so much so they would get the evil eye from Professor Randall for making too much noise during labs.

Daisy liked Tony. They started spending time together, and Daisy introduced Tony to her girlfriends; Kara, and Deni. "Tony, these are my friends, Kara and Deni. Guys, this is Tony. He's a freshman, too. He's really shy, but we're harmless, right girls?"

"Right!" Kara and Deni chimed in, laughing sneakily.

"If you can deal with us three lunatics, I'd say you can handle just about anything! We're all screwed up", Deni said jokingly. "I'm sure you'll either fit right in, or run for the hills", she said as they all burst into laughter. Tony felt very much at ease with these girls, right away, so much so, they talked him into joining the dance team; something he admitted to them that he had always loved to do.

"I love to dance" he confessed. "Even though I was on the dance team in high school, back home, I couldn't show how much I loved it, because my father would've gone ballistic! He thinks that men that dance are "sissys" and that was pretty much what he thought of me, until I told him it was a way for me to get more girls".

"Nonsense" Daisy declared with her hand on her hip and her face frowned up. "Dance is very difficult and demanding. You must be incredibly fit and disciplined, just like in any sport! I get so sick of people thinking that dance is for the weak". She stood up on the bench and said passionately "I'd like to see ANY of them get up there and train like we train and do what we do!". And training they did; lots of it.

Every day at five o'clock in the evening, the dance team was in the auditorium rehearsing. Some days they wouldn't get out of rehearsals until nine o'clock at night. Four hours of grueling training and rehearsing would wear them out and most nights, they would miss dinner in the cafeteria, so they had to eat off campus; which they didn't mind because the food on campus wasn't that great.

One night, after an incredibly brutal rehearsal, they decided to just hang out in Tony's room, since he was the only one with his own room and ordered pizza. It was the first time that any of them had been to his room and they were amazed at his style. "Whoa, Tony! I don't think I have EVER seen a guy's room look this BEAUTIFUL before!" gasped Deni, as she clutched her t-shirt, walking in the door.

"Are you sure you're a guy?" asked Daisy in a jokingly manner. Daisy, however, was highly discerning and saw the glimpse of sadness that came over his face as he looked down at the floor. "I'm sorry Tony" she said apologetically. "I was just kidding. I didn't mean to offend you. It's just that I've never seen a guy have a room like this before".

"No. I'm not offended at all" he said with an uneasiness in his voice. He tried to pretend that it didn't bother him, but deep down it did. "I'm just glad that you like it" he said after he took a deep breath as if to shake off what he was feeling.

There was color everywhere, from his deep purple comforter, his candy apple red suede cloth chaise lounge, the Ikat, Moroccan, and honeycomb throw pillows in shades of purple, red, orange, turquoise, and white, with a white shag carpet. It looked as if they had stepped into a home décor magazine. As they laid, sprawled out all over the place, the conversation went from light and full of laughter, to the point of tears, to sharing deep intimate secrets about themselves.

After a short moment of silence, after an eruption of laughter, Deni let out a huge sigh. "I wish I could just be like this and laugh all the time" she said. "When I go home" taking a deep breath, as her eyes gazed at the floor, "I never get to laugh like this. I'm never happy at home."

As Daisy placed her hand gently on Deni's shoulder, the tears started to flow from Deni's eyes. "Whenever I'm home" she sobbed "either I'm invisible or my mother criticizes me about everything; especially my weight". She wiped her eyes and just sat there in silence.

As everyone began to shed tears, the confessions just started flowing. Daisy was next. "My parents never want me to do anything" she said as she rolled her eyes. "When I'm home", she continued, "I feel like I'm in prison. They still treat me like I'm two and won't let me go anywhere. Even here" as she sat up on the floor she continued "she wants to know everything I'm doing and monitor my every move. It's like she is scared to death that something is going to happen to me, because of what happened to her when she was young".

Daisy's mother, Gina, was molested by a family member from the age of seven until she was in middle school. When Gina told her mother, her mother told her to never tell anyone that story again. Gina never trusted anyone after that and vowed that her children would never know that pain. She did everything that was in her power to shield her from ever getting hurt the way that she did; which made Daisy feel trapped. Gina was so paranoid that she would never let Daisy go anywhere where Gina wasn't. It was a wonder Gina let Daisy go away to college without trying to move with her.

Tony looked somewhat uneasy, trying to decide if he wanted them to know his secret or not. Finally, he just pulled the band aid off and, with his eyes clenched tightly, he told them the same way that he did when he told Cyprus. "I've always felt like I was a female and I have to pretend I'm masculine because my dad would lose it if he knew!".

There was silence in the room, as Tony kept his eyes closed for a minute, afraid to see the looks on their faces. He slowly opened one eye, and then the next, and all three of the girls were looking at him as if to say, "It's ok". That was exactly what they said, too.

Daisy embraced Tony and said "this is a group where there's no judgment; a safe place. We share everything here, and nothing is to ever leave this group". They all huddled around him, squeezing him tightly; Daisy, Tony, Kara, and Deni in tears. Tony had never felt so free, accepted, and truly loved for being who he was before. He had only known the ladies for such a short period of time, yet he felt so at ease telling them a secret that he had carried around for his whole life.

After they had that breakthrough, the girls and Tony, which was now considered one of the girls, were inseparable. With the encouragement that he'd received from his friends, and unbeknownst to his family, Tony had begun talking to a doctor about Male to female (M2F) gender reassignment surgery and the process. He wanted to know all the facts before making any decisions.

Dr. Zee sat Tony down and began to run through the prerequisites for having the surgery. He had to have recommendations from two mental health specialists to ensure that he was a good candidate for gender reassignment, have hormone treatment for one year, and live as what's considered his "true self" for one year, prior to getting the surgery. He wasn't quite sure he was ready for all of that, yet, however, he wanted to at least get the information he needed to take that first step.

Daisy and Deni had gone with him to his consultation and were more nervous than he was. As they waited for him to come out, sitting in the waiting room, Daisy was biting her nails and Deni was pacing back and forth until Daisy yelled at her to sit down. It seemed like he was in there for hours when the door finally opened, and it was Tony coming out, looking anxious, overwhelmed, and excited at the same time.

Deni ran over to him "Well, what did the doctor say? Are you going to go through with it?"

Daisy put her hand on Deni's shoulder as if to calm her down and said, "Why don't we just give him a chance to take it all in and process it before we bombard him with questions". Daisy was always the voice of reason and the calm one out of the bunch. That's why they called her "Mama Daisy".

Walking out to the car, it was as if Tony forgot to breathe. He was still in shock that he even had the nerve to go. Finally, once they got in the car, he exhaled, it seemed, for the longest time and told them everything the doctor had said. "I'm not sure if I'm quite ready to live as my "true self" for a whole year, yet" he said, "but maybe I could start trying for weekends when we go off campus and see how I handle that". And that is exactly what he started doing.

Every weekend, they would hit the club scene, go to the movies, go bowling, or whatever they felt like doing but were far enough away from campus, that no one would recognize them. He would dress up like a girl, put on his wig and makeup, and became Toni with an "I". He was tall and slender, not too muscular, and he was so beautiful that you couldn't tell he was a guy.

The first night he was scared out of his mind. He just knew someone would recognize him and know that he wasn't a girl, but when no one did, he became more and more comfortable. His family had no clue as to what was going on. Whenever he said he was out with Daisy or spending time with Daisy, they just assumed that she was his new girlfriend. Of course, his father couldn't have been happier; especially when he saw pictures of them together and saw how beautiful she was.

Tony was being "Toni" all semester, on the weekends. Those weekends made him feel so effervescent. By the end of that semester, he knew that he wanted to move forward with the gender reassignment surgery, but how was he going to tell his family? Would they cut him off, financially? Not pay for his college tuition anymore? Or worse; disown him. Was he ready to be on his own, without the support of his family? These were all the questions that were going through his mind. He had made up in his mind that he was going to talk to his parents when he went home for Christmas.

Arriving at the Baltimore Washington International Airport (BWI), Tony had knots all in his stomach. His mouth felt dry and his legs felt like they had cement attached to them, the further he got to where his sister Gigi and his mother were picking him up. He wondered if they would be able to notice anything different about him.

"Hey doll!" Tony said to his mom as he leaned in the window to kiss her on the cheek. Gigi got out of the car and walked around to the curb where he was, to help him with his bags. As she leaned down to grab one of the lighter bags, she reached up and brought his forehead down to kiss him like she always did. Tony was all his sisters' baby and they all acted like they were his mother, too.

When Tony, his mom, and Gigi entered the house, all the girls came running to the door to greet him; his father came, too. Everyone was already there for the holidays and he was the last to arrive. The girls were all worried that he looked too skinny and wanted to feed him.

All his father was interested in was how many girls he met and had been with. Of course, Tony lied. He wasn't quite ready to tell his family about "Toni" yet. It was too soon. *I'll tell them before I leave, for sure*, he thought to himself. He wasn't sure how things were going to go, and he didn't want to ruin anyone's Christmas. So, again, he played the game.

As the rest of the family started to arrive early Christmas morning, the house had all kinds of amazing smells from all the ladies up cooking and prepping food the night before. The aroma of honey glazed ham, smoked turkey, and the smell of the cinnamon apple candles that were lit all over the house made Tony feel nostalgic. It reminded him of the years his great grandmother, Bea was alive. She was the heart and soul of the family. She was full of fire and spunk, and she always looked fabulous. Tony always felt a special connection with her. He felt like she was the one that he was the most like.

Just like clockwork, the doorbell rang at noon, like it had every other year that Tony could remember. It was his Uncle Johnny, his Aunt Maria, and their sons Johnny, Jr. (A.K.A. JJ), Luciano (or Luke for short), and Bobby. Bobby and Luke were fraternal twins and they were the same age as Tony. JJ was the oldest of the three. They were always taller and stockier than he was and they both wrestled. Tony hated when Bobby and Luke came around because they always used him for wrestling practice while Tony's dad and uncles laughed.

Shortly after Uncle Johnny and Aunt Maria came, my mom's sister, Aunt Angela and her husband Uncle

Mike, and their daughter, Sabrina came over. Aunt Angela was beautiful, just like my mom. She had long wavy salt and pepper hair that she would wear in a slick bun, her nails were always a deep crimson that matched her signature lipstick, and she always had some amazing outfit on. Today, it was a black silk jumpsuit and leopard print stilettos with the purse to match.

Aunt Angela never came early, like Aunt Rosa did because Aunt Angela never learned how to cook. She just always hired people to cook for her dinner parties or get my mom and Aunt Rosa to cook. Whenever Tony would become "Toni", Aunt Angela was who was going to take his fashion cues from. He never saw her undone.

After dinner was over, the men were gathered in the media room, watching football, while the women were upstairs cleaning and gossiping. Tony, more than ANYTHING, wanted to be upstairs with the ladies instead of watching every dreadful second of football. They always sounded like they were having more fun.

During halftime, Uncle Bobby started talking to Tony's dad about the twins getting into trouble at school for roughing up this kid that said he was a girl now. "The boy deserved it." Uncle Bobby said passionately. He went on to say, "What is all this crap about boys being girls and girls wanting to be boys and this transgender BS?"

"Let me tell you something, Bobby" said Anthony, Sr. "If my boy came to me talking that crap, I'd take him out!! No son of mine will ever tell me he feels like a girl" he yelled. "I hope your boys beat the crap out of him!"

Anthony said. Tony couldn't believe what he was hearing, but then again, he could. He knew how his father felt about all that stuff. He wasn't shy about stating his homophobic, antiquated, and chauvinistic views at all. At that moment, Tony knew that there was no way he could ever tell his father what he was considering doing. He felt lost.

Tony ran outside, down to the water. He sat there on the edge of the yard overlooking the Chesapeake Bay. As he sat there, he listened to the waves crash against the dock and the rowboat that belonged to his parents that was sometimes used to get to the yacht. Suddenly, Tony just decided he wanted to just get away from everybody, clear his head, and try to figure out what he was going to do with his life. He knew he couldn't stay trapped and that the only way he could feel free was to be who he knew he was on the inside.

As he climbed inside the boat, with one foot he went to push himself and the boat away from the dock, but as he pushed, his foot got tangled up in the rope and he fell, hitting his head on the dock, knocking himself out cold. While he was knocked out, he saw a vision of a man. He couldn't make out his face, but all he could tell was that he was an African American. He didn't look like he was in a panic, in fact, he seemed inexplicably serene, which put Tony at ease. It started to get dark and the man slowly started drifting away, it seemed.

The next thing he remembered was waking up, coughing up water. His leg was free from the rope. He couldn't remember how he even got back on the dock. All he remembers is finding a card lying beside him that had an address, date, and time on it.

9 THE VIRTUOUS VICTIM

"I hate men!!" Jess screamed at the top of her lungs, tears streaming down her face, fist tightly clenched, face so frowned up it almost looked disfigured. She had just found out that her fiancé of two and a half years, had cheated on her with one of her closest girlfriends. She couldn't believe it!

Derrick seemed like the perfect catch. He was a successful business owner, had no kids, and had never been married, which was practically unheard of with men her age. Such a perfect gentleman, he seemed to sweep Jess right off her feet in record speed. Everything about him just seemed so right. She knew that if she didn't get him, he would not be on the market for much longer. It didn't matter to either of them that she was black and he was white. All they saw was the love in each other's eyes. At least that's what she saw...

I should've known he was too good to be true she thought to herself as she walked around with a trash can tossing all his shredded belongings that were left in her house. Out of sheer rage, Jess just ripped and cut whatever belongings that she could find of his that was still there after she smacked the fire out of him, told him that she never wanted to see him again, and threw what she could grab out the door behind him. Derrick swiftly walked down the steps, leaving her and the house that she had just bought with him, a just a little over a month prior.

Our wedding, she thought to herself, as she sat in the middle of the floor like a pile of mush and sobbed uncontrollably. *What am I going to tell everybody; all the money spent on my dress, the venue, the caterers, all the money that my bridesmaids put out for their dresses? What am I going to tell everybody; that the wedding is off because my fiancé has been sleeping with one of my best friends, right under my nose for* **months**?

As Jess had this painful dialogue in her own head, she thought of all the humiliation, let alone the pure disgust, hurt, and anger she felt. She couldn't understand how she could've been so stupid! She was extremely intelligent, she graduated in the top of her class, earned an MBA from Clark Atlanta University and started her own consulting firm at the age of twenty-seven. She was right on schedule to having the life she had always planned and dreamed of for herself.

Jess didn't come from money, initially. Her father worked for a tech company for twenty years, but when the company folded, her father decided to start his own company. He had to use all his savings to start his business. Jess just worked her way through undergrad and graduate school and she never regretted a moment of it. She never wanted her parents to help her. She felt she would appreciate it more if she worked for it, and she did.

After kissing all the frogs in her life, Jess felt like she had finally found her Prince, in Derrick. He was a prince alright. "Prince of darkness", she said out loud in a snarky tone. Now, Jess would have to start the painful process of picking up the pieces of her utterly shattered heart and figure out how she was going to get through the rest of her life without the one person she thought she'd share it with.

The first-person Jess had to break the news to, was her mother, Dawn. She knew that her mother would know how to tell her father, Jesse, in a manner that would keep him calm enough that he wouldn't want to rip his head off, she hoped. Although, somehow, she doubted there would be anything to prevent him from doing that anyway. As she pulled up to her parents' house, Jess felt a lump in her throat and that sickening feeling in the pit of her stomach. She didn't know how to even begin to explain it all.

As soon as Jess opened the door, and saw her mother standing at the kitchen counter, Jess just started bawling hysterically. She knew that her mother would know just by looking at her, that something was terribly wrong. Quickly rushing to her daughter's side, Dawn wrapped her arms around Jess, holding her head in her hands, allowing her to cry, until she could regain enough of her composure to talk.

As Jess took her mother by the hand and led her to the sofa in the family room, she took two extremely deep, purposeful breaths before saying "the wedding is off. Derrick cheated on me with one of my best friends and

God only knows who else". Feeling a sharp pain shoot through her heart, like an arrow, Dawn clutched her chest in disbelief.

"I'll kill him!" she screeched with a loud shrill voice. "How could he do such a thing?" she asked, still with her hand over her heart, as if it was her own heart that had been broken. Dawn could feel her daughter's pain. So many thoughts were going through her mind, and she had so many questions she wanted to ask, however, she didn't want to make this moment about her or what she felt. This moment was about Jess, alone. *What she must be feeling,* Dawn thought, as Jess collapsed her head onto her mother's lap.

Jess continued to mutter out the way that she found out and how she reacted to it. It all seemed like a nightmare; just surreal. It was as if the words were coming out, but they didn't sound like they were coming from her mouth. Devastation, betrayal, hurt, rage, pain were all the things that she felt at the same time. *How am I going to get through this?* she thought to herself.

Dawn stroked her daughter's beautiful, chestnut colored locks, and whispered words of comfort in her ear, as Jess laid in her lap; not knowing what her mother was saying because she didn't want to hear it. At that moment, Jess just wanted to be numb, and she was until she just drifted off to sleep; her body limp from exhaustion. Dawn slid from underneath her daughter and covered her with a blanket and went off to bed.

As the sunlight pierced through the blinds, Jess cracked her right eye open, not wanting to expose herself to the full strength of it. Not really wanting to get up, but the smell of crisp turkey bacon, whole wheat waffles, and coffee alerted her that her father would probably be coming down for breakfast soon, and that she would have to prepare herself to tell him what happened.

Their private chef, Tristen, was in the kitchen preparing breakfast as she'd done for the past five years, since Jess's father had a heart attack. Jesse was always exercising, and they thought he was taking good care of himself because he always looked like he was in good shape, but he would still eat all the wrong things and had quite a bit of stress in his life. That scared Dawn enough to decide that she needed some help with teaching them how to eat healthy, so when Tristen lost her job working for one of their favorite restaurants, they decided to hire her to be their full-time private chef.

"Good morning, Jess", Tristan beamed, "it's not often that we get to see you out here. How's everything going", she asked. Not wanting to disclose any information as to why she was there, nor wanting to even think about the situation at the time, Jess just put on the face that she's been known to put on when she wants to pretend that she has it altogether and let out a "everything is good" lie. She was cool with Tristan, but they were around the same age and traveled in some of the same circles. Jess wasn't ready for this news to get out, prematurely.

"Are you hungry?" Tristen asked, as she motioned to the food that was laid out on the kitchen counter.

"Just some fruit, please" Jess requested. "I don't have much of an appetite".

"Fresh fruit, it is". Tristan slid a bowl in front of Jess filled with fresh, plump strawberries, cantaloupe, honey dew, and pineapples. As Jess sat there, eating her fruit in silence, while Tristan continued to prepare breakfast, in walked Jesse. Surprised to see his daughter sitting at the counter, he stopped for a second, and knowing his daughter, said "What did Derrick do?".

"Good morning to you, too, daddy, and nothing" as she turned back around rolling her eyes, trying her best to fight the tears that she could feel wanting to well up. He could always see right through her, so she knew she couldn't look directly at him. Jesse walked over, bent down, and gently placed a kiss on her forehead.

Jess just melts in her daddy's arms whenever he's around. He makes her feel safe, makes everything better, but this, he couldn't fix and if she told him, she would be visiting him behind bars. She knew she would eventually have to tell him, though, or he would hear it from someone else, and it would be ten times worse. She grabbed his hand, led him into his office and asked him to sit down.

"It's that bad that I have to sit?" he asked, clenching his fists.

"Daddy, please," she looked at him with those puppy dog eyes that he could never resist. "I just need you to remain calm and just listen to me", she said in a very still tone; the kind of tone that one would use when not trying to wake a sleeping bear. "The wedding is off" she continued.

Jesse jumped up out of his seat and yelled "I'll kill him! I knew you shouldn't have trusted that scrawny little white boy!" he shouted. Jesse started to head out of the kitchen, but Jess ran behind him, grabbed his arm and pulled him back.

"Daddy, it's for the best!" she tried to explain to him, but he couldn't hear over his fury.

Dawn came running down the stairs, as she heard all the commotion. She realized that Jess must've told her father what happened, and yelled "Jesse Bartholomew Tate!", as she grabbed him and spun him around. Dawn looked him dead in his eyes and said in a shrewd voice "Don't you dare go out that door! Your daughter is a grown woman and can handle her own business". As Jesse attempted to form a rebuttal, Dawn continued to say in a sharp tone "If you go starting trouble and get locked up, I'm leaving you there!"

Thinking about how foolish and reckless it would be to go over to Derrick's house and beat the boy down, Jesse stopped, turned around slowly, and just stared at his daughter. He could see the fear in her eyes and realized that the last thing she needed was a hot-headed father that escalated the situation and added more stress to this already horrendous situation. Jesse just walked over to his daughter and wrapped his arms around her and softly whispered in her ear "Daddy's got you, baby girl". That was all she needed to hear.

Weeks went by and Jess started to feel semi-normal again, after she had taken two weeks off work and went away on a Mediterranean cruise by herself. She didn't want to be bothered with anyone. All she wanted was to go away where no one knew her, with a little bit of peace and solitude; alone with her thoughts, time for prayer, and meditation; just her and God. It was everything she needed. She started to feel like herself again, and amidst all the glances and whispers from her employees as she walked through the building to her office, surprisingly, she felt at peace.

A few months went by and Jess was feeling mentally and emotionally stronger than she had ever felt before. Her life seemed to be back on track. She had even considered possibly trying to date again, then suddenly, out of nowhere, she started to feel unusually drained. Although she was taking her vitamins, eating healthy, and working out regularly, something just wasn't feeling right in her body.

As she made an appointment with her doctor, Jess just shrugged it off, figuring it was nothing but that her body was just coming down off all the recent stress and anxiety from the whole Derrick situation, but she wanted to get checked out to make sure. The doctor ordered routine blood work to check to see if maybe she was Vitamin D, Vitamin B12, or Iron deficient, and to check her white blood count and urine to ensure that there were no infections or viruses of any kind that she had contracted being out of the country. He also wanted to rule out pregnancy, since Jess's cycle was irregular, and she hadn't had a period in a while. She just assumed it was stress, certainly not pregnancy. *God wouldn't be that cruel*, she thought to herself.

About four days later, Jess's doctor's office called her and wanted her to come back in for some more tests. The doctor had some concerns from the results of the blood work and urine sample that they took. Jess started to be somewhat concerned, but just thought that maybe she did contract a virus or something; still thinking it wasn't anything major.

"Sit down, Miss Tate" the doctor motioned for her to sit in the chair against the wall. "The reason that I called you in, is because there was blood in your urine sample and when asked when your last menstrual cycle was, you stated that it had been over a couple of months and the pregnancy test was negative." Flipping through Jess's charts, he continued "Your white blood cells are elevated, which means that your body is fighting off some foreign matter. You are also running a slight fever, and today, your blood pressure is slightly elevated. Have you been running fevers?" Dr. Chin asked.

"Honestly, doctor, I haven't even paid attention. I just know I have felt run down and can't seem to get warm enough". Starting to really get nervous, Jess asked "Doctor, what is it? What do you think is going on with me?"

"Well, I don't want you to be frightened or worried, right now" he said as he saw the look on her face and did not want her to become panicked. "I just want to run one more test."

"O-ok" Jess stammered. "What is the test and when do I need to get it done?"

"Have you ever heard of an Intravenous Pyelogram or an IVP?" he asked.

"No. What is that?" Jess asked with her face frowned up. It sounded like it was serious, painful, and something that she was not interested in doing.

"It is a type of x-ray of your kidneys. Dye is injected and travels to your urinary tract to highlight any possible tumors" explained Dr. Chin.

"T-tumors?" she asked with a ghostly look on her face. "As in cancer?"

"We don't want to label it just yet, Ms. Tate. We just want to make sure we check for everything and to rule some things out". As he put down her chart and looked Jess in the eye, he placed his hand on top of hers, as to calm her wrecked nerves and said, "Let's just take it one step at a time and see what we're working with, before we make any rash decisions".

Dr. Chin got up out of his chair and walked around his desk to help Jess up. He walked with her to the front desk and said "My receptionist will give you the script to have the test completed. You can call and schedule an appointment". As Dr. Chin and Jess walked to the door for her to go back into the lobby, he said to her in a stern voice "I strongly urge you to have this test done as soon as possible. The sooner we can diagnose you and start to treat whatever this is, the better".

The next few days waiting for the test results were some of the most excruciating days of her life. She told only her parents of the suspicions that the doctor had. She didn't want anyone around already diagnosing her with cancer and having her already on her death bed, before the results even came in. She had to stay in faith or she felt like she would just crumble under the weight of it all and then, finally, she got the call that she had been waiting for, one evening while she was working late.

Dr. Chin called Jess, himself, requesting that she come to the office first thing in the morning to discuss the results of the test. She knew that that wasn't a good sign. If the results were negative, he would have just told her over the phone or sent her a letter or had his nurse contact her. He certainly wouldn't be calling and asking her to come in right away.

Jess just got up from her desk, left everything that she was working on right where it was, and walked to the empty parking lot where her car was parked. When she got to the door of the car, before she got in, she felt like she was about to have a panic attack. She just stood there for a moment and tried to take some deep breaths. As she looked up at the sky, she began yelling at the top of her lungs, "God, how can this be happening to me on top of EVERYTHING ELSE that I have been through?".

Leaning over the roof of the car, weeping overwhelmingly, Jess continued her rant and questioned God. "I've done right by you! I haven't slept around. I treated people right. I stayed in church and tried to serve you the best way that I could. I prayed, fasted, studied your word, and believed in you! What did I do to deserve this?", she cried. "Am I just cursed? Do you even love me?".

After finally getting enough strength to open the door and get in the car, she sunk down in the seat, and began to get angry. What do I have to live for? She began to think to herself. *God is trying to take everything from me. First, I lose the man that I thought He sent me to my best friend.* The more she thought about it, the angrier she became. *I got embarrassed, and ridiculed. On the verge of losing this four-bedroom home that we just purchased because we wanted to start a family right away. I thought I was going to have help paying for it, and **NOW** I could possibly be losing my **LIFE**?"* she thought to herself as the tears just vehemently streamed down her face.

Emotionally, Jess was spinning out of control fast, and was speeding down the highway even faster. As the rain started to come down, Jess's vision started to become even more impaired than the tears alone were making them. She tried to wipe her eyes so that she could see more clearly, but as she took her sleeve to wipe her eyes, a car came out of nowhere and side swiped her. All Jess could do was scream the name "JESUS" before she blacked out. While she was out, she heard someone in her ear saying very clearly, "It's not your time yet, Beautiful. There's more for you to do. Stay with me".

In that instance, Jess gasped for breath, clutching her chest. It felt as if it was exploding! She looked beside her and saw nothing but a bright light shining in her face, and broken glass in the passenger's seat.

"Ma'am are you ok?". When Jess opened her eyes, she saw this beautiful, tall, dark skinned brotha staring down at her. He was holding her head in his hand and telling her not to move. Jess thought to herself "Is this man an angel?". She turned red with embarrassment after realizing that she spoke her thoughts out loud, when he answered back "Ummmm... No. I just witnessed the accident and called for help". "Just try not to move. The EMT's are here".

After two days of being in the hospital, with no major injuries, Jess was discharged. Although her parents wanted her to come home with them, Jess just wanted to go home to her own bed. She had so much to process. While in the hospital, Dr. Chin, who also worked in the hospital, visited her and discussed the results of her tests. Dr. Chin just confirmed what she already knew, she had cancer; kidney cancer.

"The good news", stated Dr. Chin, as he placed his hand on her shoulder as to assure her that there was good news, "is that it is Stage 1 and the tumor is only one and three quarters of an inch in diameter. Due to the tumor being small and confined to the kidney, only, it can be removed through a procedure called a partial nephrectomy. This will remove the tumor laparoscopically which reduces your recovery time from six to eight weeks, to two and a half weeks".

As Jess lay on her couch, trying not to think of all that was ahead of her, and how she did not have Derrick there to be with her through all of this, she heard the doorbell ring. She slowly shuffled to the door in her favorite fleece pajamas and fuzzy slipper socks, opened the door to find her baby sister, Kimberly, standing there.

It had been about three years or more since Jess had seen or heard from her sister, but in that moment, she did not care. She missed her sister and when Kimberly left home, Jess was away at college. She had never contacted Jess to tell her where she was or how she was doing. Jess didn't even know how Kimberly knew how to find her. She was just happy that she showed up on her doorstep, right at that moment.

As they stood at the door and holding on to each other for dear life, for what seemed to be forever, with tears in their eyes, Jess just held Kimberly's face in her hands. "Look at you!" she cried. "You're just all grown up, now." As Jess led Kimberly into the apartment, Kimberly just kept staring at her sister in disbelief.

"I've missed you so much, sis!" she said, as she just dropped to her knees crying hysterically.

Jess quickly went into big sister mode "What happened? What's Wrong" she cried, as she slowly sat on the floor beside her sister and began to rock her. It was at that moment that Jess realized that both Tate sisters had been through quite a bit of heartbreak.

After a couple of days of catching up and just being sisters again, it was just like old times. They sat around in their pjs, eating and watching movies. After a while, Jess began to share what she had been going through, recently, with Derrick, the wedding, and cancer that she had just been diagnosed with.

Kimberly felt so bad for her sister. She was the one that always did right. Kimberly was the black sheep of the family. She expected bad things to happen to her, but they weren't supposed to happen to Jess.

After Kimberly, hugged Jess and let her cry, she began to tell Jess about the daughter that she had, how she had been homeless and stealing, been raped and everything, until she got involved in stripping, and how she was beat within inches of her life. She pulled out this business card. She began to tell Jess about how this man had saved her life and how he left that card with the date, address, and time on it. She also told Jess that for some reason, she felt led to share it with her, and that she thought that the reason she was led there, was because Jess needed to go with her.

"I don't know about that" Jess said, shaking her head, in disagreement. "What if it's a satanic cult or something" Jess asked. "What if it's a sex trafficking ring?"

she continued. "It could be dangerous and I'm dealing with a lot, right now" Jess said, still shaking her head "no".

"If it was a sex trafficking ring, they could've just gotten me at the club. Rick was involved in all of that", she said. "Jess. You know how we were raised. You know that God gave me great discernment, and while I've been out of the church and have felt so far from Him these days, I still have that gift". Kimberly persistently tried to convince her sister, giving her that look she always gave her when they were younger, when Kimberly wanted to get her way. "I really do think it was God that led me to you, and He wants me to take you, with me. I really think this is for both of us. Whatever it is" she pleaded.

As crazy as it sounded and seemed. There was something about it that intrigued Jess. She knew that Kimberly was right. Whenever Kimberly had a bad feeling or a good feeling about something, since she was a little girl, she was always right. Maybe this would be the miracle that she had been praying for.

"When is this thing and where is your daughter?" Jess asked, trying to avoid answering.

Kimberly stated "The card says: **101 Front St, NW, Baltimore, January 3, 2019 6:00 PM.** That's tomorrow night and to answer your question, my daughter is staying with her godmother until I can get on my feet. I didn't want her life to be disrupted, again. So, we're going?" Kimberly asked impatiently.

Jess rolled her eyes and reluctantly said "Yes. I will go with you and after that, we're going to go get your daughter. You two can stay with me for a while. I have plenty of room." The two sisters hugged one another and continued to laugh and joke with each other and it felt just like old times.

10 I AM CALEB

As the motley crew got closer to the address that was on the card, it seemed as if everyone's pace had slowed down. There was, what appeared to be a silhouette of a woman in the alley, slumped over. As they got closer, they could see a needle sticking out of her arm. "Is she getting high right on the street?" Daisy asked Tony in disbelief. She had only witnessed people getting high on television; never in real life.

Daisy was scared, and she wasn't the only one. As they walked by her, the woman barely even looked up at them. She was just sitting there, in a daze, looking like a zombie; like there was no life left in her. Her eyes started to roll up into the back of her head and she just laid her head down on a bag of trash that someone had thrown out in the alley. *How could someone live like that*, Daisy wondered to herself. She thought her life was rough but was quickly reminded that it could be much worse.

No one seemed to want to open the door, afraid of what may be behind it, they all just stood there staring at each other, and staring back at the door. "Whose going in first?" Deni asked.

"I'm not" said Bryce as he took a step back. "This could be a whole setup to have us all killed", he said as he was shaking his head "no". The "white guy" that looked "hot" to Deni, walked up to the door and snatched it open.

"Man, y'all are a bunch of punks" he said. "I'm going in and getting this over with. This had better be worth my time!" he said, annoyed that he had to be there with all of them. Although he was pretending that he wasn't afraid, he was terrified, but he thought Deni was cute and didn't want to embarrass himself in front of her.

As he opened the door, they all peeked inside, and it was dark, old, and dingy. There were a bunch of large objects covered with black tarps, but no one could tell what was underneath of them. As they inched their way in, closely knitted together in a huddle, not caring about their differences at that time, they were looking around against the walls to see if they could find a light to turn on. Suddenly, a bright light shone in the middle of the room on a stage, down onto the silhouette of a man.

This man, dressed in all black, was stocky, tall, and had a menacing look on his face. If they weren't afraid before, they were afraid now. They just knew they were all about to be slaughtered like in some crazy horror film. They stood there frozen, as the man summoned them with his hands to come closer, no one wanted to move. He summoned them again, stating "I promise, I come in peace" opening his arms wide, as if he were about to give them a hug. Although he looked scary, there seemed to be something about him that seemed eerily familiar and serene.

Slowly moving forward, Bryce broke away from the crowd, as he was the first to notice who he was. "Hey, you're the man that saved me in the alley" he said while pointing at him. "I couldn't remember your face, but it was something about your eyes when you looked in the rearview mirror, that I would never forget". As he moved closer, unafraid, the rest of them started to let their guards down and began to move forward, as well. "Who are you and why are we here?", Bryce asked.

As Caleb jumped down from the stage, he said in an eerily deep and robust voice "I am Caleb. You are about to embark on a journey unlike one you have ever been on before, should you accept this assignment". Everyone looked around at each other wondering what assignment he was talking about. Some were captivated, some were anxious, thinking that this may be some sort of cult. Out of nowhere, an equally menacing and towering giant came forward from behind Caleb and said "I have already accepted the assignment. I promise you, what we're about to embark on will change the whole trajectory of not only your life, but the lives of many others. Will you join us?" he asked as he held out his hand.

ABOUT THE AUTHOR

Tamara Chanelle Miller worked in the field of Social Work and Education for the past fifteen years, with BA and MA degrees in Psychology, she has been exposed to many individuals from all different walks of life. Growing up in the small town of Chester, MD, on a little Island called Kent Island, and traveling all over the globe, Tamara has heard thousands of stories from those that have been at their lowest, most despondent moments in life, and has always desired to be a catalyst for hope and encouragement. Tamara spent most of her time growing up in the church, and her faith is what has provided her with the ability to navigate through the difficult waters of her own life. She has dealt with and overcome severe depression, anxiety, as well as insecurity and believes that she has done so with the mandate to help those that are suffering from those same issues. *The Caleb Movement* series is how she plans to begin to fulfill that call. Tamara is currently residing in Bensalem, Pennsylvania, with her husband, Phil Miller.

39512228R00093

Made in the USA
Middletown, DE
19 March 2019